**San**

Along with her other bad habits, she'd acquired a new one since meeting Jack Martin. Now her active imagination included mechanical drawings and... weddings.

A shiver raced down her spine. Samantha wrapped her arms across her chest. She had to physically hold herself together or the self-image she'd constructed of being a self-sufficient, independent woman would explode into a zillion pieces.

Much as she wanted to ignore the fact that she was a woman with normal physical urges, she couldn't. By closing her eyes, she could recall each moment of the previous night. Her traitorous body had taken notes far more carefully than those she entered in her inventor's log.

Dear Reader,

Welcome to Silhouette! Our goal is to give you hours of unbeatable reading pleasure, and we hope you'll enjoy each month's six new Silhouette Desires. These sensual, provocative love stories are both believable and compelling—sometimes they're poignant, sometimes humorous, but always enjoyable.

Indulge yourself. Experience all the passion and excitement of falling in love along with our heroine as she meets the irresistible man of her dreams and together they overcome all obstacles in the path to a happy ending.

If this is your first Desire, I hope it'll be the first of many. If you're already a Silhouette Desire reader, thanks for your support! Look for some of your favorite authors in the coming months: Stephanie James, Diana Palmer, Dixie Browning, Ann Major and Doreen Owens Malek, to name just a few.

Happy reading!

Isabel Swift
Senior Editor

SDRL-7/85

# JO ANN ALGERMISSEN
## Serendipity Samantha

Silhouette Desire

Published by Silhouette Books New York

**America's Publisher of Contemporary Romance**

**SILHOUETTE BOOKS**
300 East 42nd St., New York, N.Y. 10017

Copyright © 1986 by Jo Ann Algermissen

All rights reserved, including the right to reproduce
this book or portions thereof in any form whatsoever.
For information address Silhouette Books,
300 East 42nd St., New York, N.Y. 10017

ISBN: 0-373-05300-2

First Silhouette Books printing August 1986

America's Publisher of Contemporary Romance

Printed in the U.S.A.

**Books by Jo Ann Algermissen**

Silhouette Desire

*Naughty, but Nice* #246
*Challenge the Fates* #276
*Serendipity Samantha* #300

## JO ANN ALGERMISSEN

believes in love, be it romantic love, sibling love, parental love or love of books. She's given and received them all. Ms. Algermissen and her husband of twenty years live on Kiawah Island in South Carolina with their two children, a weimaraner and three horses. She considers herself one lucky lady. Jo Ann also writes under, the pseudonym Anna Hudson.

Dedicated with sisterly love to Jack Hudson,
for understanding and practising
Dad's concept of *family*.

# One

——

With her million-dollar idea wrapped in plastic and tucked firmly under her arm, Samantha Mason impatiently glanced at the main gate leading into Astro Hall. She looked over her shoulder. There were long aisles of fishing paraphernalia, with everything from sinkers to canoes on display.

Houston, Texas hosted one of the finest outdoorsmen shows in the nation. Samantha planned on capitalizing on the opportunity for hundreds of people to see her invention. Texans considered the Astrodome, which was next door, the eighth wonder of the world. SAM trunks would be the ninth—if Jacob arrived.

"Where is he?" she muttered.

Jacob Klein was supposed to have been there half an hour ago. Samantha checked her watch for the tenth time in the same number of seconds. She had exactly twenty-seven minutes to get Jacob appropriately attired to jump into the swimming pool-sized tank of water used for demonstrating fishing equipment. She wouldn't get another opportunity for a live demonstration of *her* invention until next year's Boat and Fishing Show.

Samantha was ready. Beneath her vivacious pink jogging suit edged with white piping, she wore the female version of the swimsuit that could ultimately save lives throughout the United States. For that matter, throughout the world.

*Texas is waiting for my invention,* she thought, gritting her teeth, *and Jacob is probably stuck in the Houston traffic!* She had all she could do to keep herself from grabbing the first man who would fit into the swimming trunks and shoving him into the tank.

The thought made her scalp tingle. She fluffed her short, curly blond hair as though a flash of genius—that stroke of brilliance which the U.S. patent office requires before granting a patent—had electrically charged each silky strand. Her blue eyes, which had been glued to the turnstiles, now scrutinized the males passing down the aisles, for height, weight and physical attractiveness. For the flotation device to work, the man had to be close to Jacob's measurements.

"There has to be *someone* around here I can convince to model SAM trunks!" she whispered aloud.

Samantha approached a couple of men who filled the bill perfectly. They were dressed in what she laughingly called "Texas tuxedos," which consisted of faded jeans, western-style plaid shirts and, topping their longish hair, straw cowboy hats. She felt certain one of them would make a perfect demonstrator.

"Howdy, fellas. My name's Sam," she greeted them, grinning broadly, her blue eyes dancing from one man to the other. Appealing to their Code of the West chivalry, she asked, "Could you help a lady in distress?"

The taller of the two doffed his hat. "Well, hello there. I'm Billy Joe, and that there's Mac. Ma'am, we'd consider it a real privilege to help you."

Samantha inwardly squirmed at the way Billy Joe's eyes appeared to be stuck to the front of her jogging suit.

"Yes, well, ah, I need . . ."

"We know just what you *need*, lady," Mac sniggered, hooking his thumbs in his wide leather belt. "And we aim to please."

"I think you've misunderstood," Samantha asserted. She protectively crossed her arms over her chest. Her million-dollar invention threatened to slip from beneath her arm. Deftly catching it with one hand, she held the plastic sack toward Billy Joe.

"Would you mind putting on this pair of swim trunks and jumping into that tank over there?"

Both men glanced toward the tank. Mac gestured toward the steps leading to the wide spectator platform built around it. "The pool they're settin' up for the casting tournament?"

Samantha nodded, aware that Billy Joe seemed to be looking for something.

"You from *Eyewitness News*? Some local newslady er somethin'?"

"Sounds more like a *Candid Camera* setup to me," Mac mumbled loud enough for Samantha to hear. "Maybe a Marvin Zindler exposé."

"Gentlemen, I'm not with a television station. I'm simply trying to find someone to demonstrate this nifty invention of mine. Hopefully, with all the major manufacturers of lifesaving vests here, one of them will see how effective it is and—"

"Come on, lady. You want one of us to jump in that pool . . . fer nuthin'? You gotta be crazy! In two seconds flat the security guards would be haulin' our ass out of there, then kickin' it out the front door. I ain't gonna do sumpthin' fer nuthin'." Mac shook his head and nudged his partner down the aisle.

"Wait a minutes fellas. I'll pay you!"

Billy Joe glanced back at her, then muttered something Samantha couldn't hear that had Mac clapping his buddy on the shoulders. She didn't have to know what had been said once she'd glanced at the people closer to those two. They were glaring at her as though she'd strolled in from Main Street. And she'd confirmed the bystanders' suspicions by offering to pay *them* when the men had refused to pay her.

She turned her back to keep her tormentors from seeing her face match the color of her jogging suit. "Men! I'd like to throttle the entire gender, starting with Jacob Klein!"

Another glance at the turnstile and one at her watch told her Jacob wasn't going to make it. She'd wasted five precious minutes.

*Insistent persistence,* she thought, reiterating the phrase that kept her going, even during the worst of times. *Get yourself another man.*

"Hey! Lady!"

Samantha wheeled around. A salesman behind a counter stacked with life jackets motioned for her to come over. She sized him up, then shook her head. He was too short. The spare tire hanging over his belt would distract from the design of the swimsuit.

Flashing him a smile of gratitude, she continued searching for someone Jacob's size.

"C'mon, lady," the salesman coaxed. "I'm from out of town."

Lord have mercy, had everyone around her heard Billy Joe and Mac?

"No, thanks," she called. "I'm looking for someone who can't swim."

"*Kinky!* Kinky lady!" His appreciative glance, followed by the words "I know someone who can't swim," had her bouncing impatiently from one foot to the other.

The stranger obviously assumed she'd politely turned him down, but knew someone who'd appreciate her offbeat version of woman's oldest profession. Time was marching on and she wasn't getting anywhere... Impulsively she marched toward the salesman.

"Who do you know who doesn't swim?" she demanded in a no-nonsense voice. "I've got twenty minutes—"

"My boss." He gestured toward a tall dark-haired man who was busy straightening the foam-filled jackets on a circular rack. "Jack Martin."

Those broad shoulders and long, muscular legs were the physique of a natural born swimmer, she thought, wondering if this glib salesman was setting her up with his boss. Samantha hadn't been born yesterday.

"You're sure he doesn't know how to swim?" she asked skeptically. "I'm not interested in any other... sport."

The salesman laughed and Samantha couldn't tell whether his rumbling chuckle was lewd or merely friendly. "Trust me. He's just what you're looking for."

"I'm straight," she stated, correcting his idea that she was kinky. "What I need is a man—"

"I heard what you need. Jack is it."

Samantha was getting sick and tired of men who asserted themselves by not letting her finish her sentences.

"You're wasting precious time," the salesman added, pointing to the round clock on the wall behind them. "Want me to introduce you?"

Full-fledged panic took hold of her as the sweeping second hand passed twelve, and the minute hand advanced. This was her last chance. She had to take it.

"I'd appreciate it."

The salesman stepped from behind the counter, touched her lightly on the elbow and directed her toward Jack Martin.

Jack shoved a size large vest in its proper place on the rack. He'd unobtrusively watched the encounter between Ned Slater and the dazzling blonde, and suspected what was about to take place. Though Ned gave the impression of being the jovial, helpful-neighbor-next-door type, Jack knew Ned to be a first-class womanizer. Not to mention superambitious. To Ned's way of thinking, the fastest way to climb the corporate ladder was to procure nubile, innocent-looking delights to tempt the boss's palate. Disgust coated Jack's tongue.

After watching her ply her trade with the two cowboys, then letting Ned escort her in his direction, there wasn't any doubt in Jack's mind as to exactly what had been arranged.

The only thing that would save Ned from being fired right on the spot was his sales record. More life jackets were being sold in Ned's southeastern territory than any other district in the nation. The bottom line at O'Toole

Life Preservers, Inc., was money. Why couldn't Ned realize introducing him to some—his mind searched for a polite word—floozy, wasn't necessary.

Meticulous by nature, Jack zipped an open vest together, avoiding having to face Ned.

"Hey, Jack. This little lady wants to meet you." Ned slapped Jack on the back and strolled back to the counter.

"What size?" Jack growled, deciding to avoid Ned's ploy by acting as through this floozy wanted a life jacket.

Grateful that Jack Martin had apparently overheard her telling the cowboys about the swim trunks, she opened her sack and reached inside as she answered, "Large."

Slightly embarrassed by her frankness, Jack snapped, "I don't think I have anything you'd be interested in."

"You'll be perfect. At this point, I can't be choosy."

From the corner of his eye, Jack observed her sizing him up and down. To hell with saving face by pretending to sell her a life jacket, he thought, grimacing. He'd be as blunt as she was.

"I'm not interested."

"Why not? Ned said—"

"Forget what Ned said. *You'd* have to pay *me*!"

For half a second Samantha longed for the good old days when a man helped a woman without expecting cash on the barrel. After all, she only had a twenty-dollar bill in her purse. Of course he wouldn't know that, she reasoned. "Okay. I'll pay you twenty dollars. Don't haggle. That's my top dollar."

Jack could feel the back of his neck turning bright red. "Lady, you're embarrassing me."

"Don't be embarrassed. Lots of men your age don't know how." Putting the sack on the concrete floor, Samantha dropped to her haunches to dig in it to find her wallet. "What I have in here will support you. Don't be scared."

"Scared?" No wonder those other men had flatly rejected her. Even his healthy male ego was taking a beating.

"You'll be perfectly safe. I'll save you if anything goes wrong," she said, stretching the truth. The reason she'd invented the fabric and designed the swimsuits was that she couldn't swim a stroke.

Jack couldn't believe his ears. This had to be the most brazen, outspoken proposition on record—a real *Guinness Book of World Records* contender. Not only was she going to pay him, she was going to provide the contraceptives!

Gracefully rising, Samantha stuck the twenty in his shirt pocket. "You'll have to undress here."

"Here? In front of God and half of Houston?" His voice cracked in the middle of the last vowel.

Samantha handed him the swim trunks. "You don't think I'm going to let you blithely steal these, do you?"

"Lady, you're crazy!" Jack shook his head as he stepped away from her.

"Not crazy, desperate."

"That too!" Jack agreed. Much to his own despair, he found himself muttering the age-old phrase: "What's a nice girl like you doing in a place like this?"

"Can you think of a better place? Look around you. Every sportsman here is a potential customer."

"A woman with your looks should be—"

"Let's not get personal." Samantha smiled. It felt good to be the one doing the interrupting for a change.

"You're going to have to hurry. We have exactly four-teen minutes to get into that tank before the fishermen start casting their lures."

"What are you? Some kind of exhibitionist?"

"I can't afford a booth for my display. It's tough enough just making ends meet."

Jack groaned aloud at her lousy puns. Ned had called her kinky, but this was way beyond kinky. Hell, he didn't even know her name and yet she expected him to make love to her in a swimming pool surrounded by gawkers? Any male who could do that was a helluva man!

"I can't do it," he muttered.

"Please," Samantha pleaded, pushing the trunks into his hand. "I won't have another opportunity like this until the next boat show."

Small currents of awareness charged from beneath her fingertip and up his arm to the region surrounding his heart. Her bright turquoise eyes enticed him. For the first time, he looked at her. Really looked at her.

His dark eyes fanned across her heart-shaped face, her perky uptilted nose, her unruly, curly hair. An aura of innocence surrounded her face.

Had he been blinded by his assumption that Ned had made an illicit arrangement? Could he have been wrong about her being a hooker?

As though he had an instant replay button in his brain, he recalled exactly what she had said. His eyes narrowed as they dropped to the swimsuit she was pressing into his hands. Within an instant, he realized his mistake. Chagrined, he started to apologize. An apology wouldn't suffice.

"What's your name?" he asked, attempting to start all over.

Samantha felt herself being sucked inside the black centers of his eyes. Her mouth became parched. "Samantha Ann Mason, Sam."

"Exactly what do you want me to do, Sam?" he asked cautiously, hedging his bets against being wrong again.

Her previously agile tongue seemed to be twisted into a knot. As though hypnotized, she droned, "I want you to put on these trunks. They're made of a revolutionary new fabric. When wet, it has the same buoyancy as six inches of foam rubber. After I announce what's going to be demonstrated, I want you to jump into the tank of water."

"And that's all?"

She slowly nodded her head up and down.

"But you won't trust me to go to the men's room and change into these?"

Her head changed direction, moving from left to right.

"You're afraid I'll steal your invention?"

Remembering how another invention had been stolen snapped Samantha from her hypnotic trance. "Couldn't you slip into the center of that rack and change?"

"You can trust me, Sam."

"I don't trust any man," she declared firmly. "That twenty in your pocket didn't grow on a money tree, though heaven knows, I'd invent one if I could! Are you going to live up to your end of the bargain or not?"

Ashamed of himself for allowing her to give him the money to begin with, he plucked it from his pocket and tried to return it to her. Samantha shrank back, sticking her hands behind her.

Jack closed the gap between them. "I don't want your money."

"You took it when you agreed to demonstrate the swimming trunks."

The green bill seemed to burn his fingers. Jack searched her pink jogging suit for a pocket. There were none. Only the partially opened zipper, which allowed a small expanse of creamy white skin to be seen, provided a place for him to tuck the bill. As wary of men as Sam was, he knew she'd slap his face if he reached toward her lush breasts.

"Let's renegotiate. I'll jump in the tank if you'll take back the twenty and have dinner with me."

Samantha grinned. Peanut butter and jelly was one heck of a lot cheaper than twenty bucks! Deftly she removed several vests from the rack to make room for him to climb into the center. "Jack Martin, you've made yourself a deal."

"Have you tested these?" he asked skeptically as he stepped over the frame to the inside.

"Of course. Once you hit the water, all you have to do is relax, bring your arms up to shoulder height and spread your legs apart," she explained.

She joined Jack in the open center of the rack and hung the vests back in place to block the view. She unzipped the top of her jogging suit, then wiggled the pants over her hips.

Jack's fingers fumbled with his shirt buttons as he watched her disrobe. His highly organized, analytical mind tried to put things in logical order. First of all, inventors were supposed to be little old gray-haired men with scraggly whiskers. Second, inventors weren't supposed to have curves a centerfold model would envy. And third, inventors with this woman's angelic face and voluptuous figure should never be called Sam. That was like naming a French poodle Killer.

"Samantha." Her full name rolled off his tongue like warm sweet honey.

"Yes?"

Jack blinked. He hadn't realized he'd spoken her name out loud. The sight of her breasts swaying as she straightened did wild things to his pulse.

"You aren't undressing. Only women are entitled to change their minds," she teased. "Shake a leg, Mr. Martin."

Samantha swallowed hard when he peeled off his shirt. His supple, tanned skin rippled over taut muscles. When she heard the change in his pockets hit the concrete floor, her eyes were drawn downward. She stifled a small, feminine gasp. Magnificent physique, she thought—absolutely, positively, magnificent.

"I think there is a design problem with these trunks," Jack commented as he pulled them on over his underwear. "O'Toole's lifesaving vests support a swimmer's head and chest."

"So?" The monosyllabic word rounded her lips to a provocative invitation.

"Well, uh—" Jack brushed the back of his hand across his mouth, then removed enough jackets to allow passage "—it stands to reason that these trunks will pop to the surface the same way the vest does, right? In case you aren't familiar with the male anatomy, I can't breath through the seat of my pants."

"I told you this invention will revolutionize the life jacket industry."

He moved closer. *Revolutionize. Change.* Jack wondered if he could change her distrust of men to complete trust in him. Along the same lines, he also wondered how her lips would taste.

Sam could hardly breath herself. The sinking, suffocating feeling that she was drowning in the dark pools of his eyes left her gasping for air.

An emergency warning bell clanged in the back of her head, reminding her that though men admired her figure, they quickly lost interest when her creative drive took precedence over physical attraction. The warning had the effect of icicles dropped down the front of her suit.

"Trust me. The trunks work," she coolly reassured him. "I don't suppose you'd consider leaving your wing-tip shoes on, would you?"

"The water would ruin them." Jack hastily took them off before she could convince him to do otherwise.

"Fishermen who fall out of their boats don't have time to remove their shoes." Samantha shrugged. "Never mind. The water won't ruin my sneakers. Ready?"

"I can almost taste a home-cooked dinner." *And two very kissable lips,* he added silently.

As they climbed the wooden ramp leading to the platform surrounding the pool, Samantha explained what she wanted him to do. While she commandeered the cordless microphone to announce the sneak preview of *Sav-A-Man*, SAM, trunks, Jack would parade the length of the platform. When she raised both hands, he would jump into the ten-foot-deep pool. Seconds later, she would join him in the water.

"Got it?" she asked, pausing at the top of the ramp.

"You will save me if my rear pops up instead of my head, won't you?"

"It won't. I promise. Well, break a leg," she said in theatrical fashion.

Samantha threw back her shoulders, pasted a showgirl smile on her face and strode to the audio table. Her stomach somersaulted with each step, but no one stopped her. She waved, smiled, blew kisses and nodded her head in the manner of a television personality making a guest appearance.

A shrill chorus of wolf whistles and catcalls followed her progress.

"Hi there," she said, stopping in front of a khaki-uniformed man who held a cordless microphone in his hand. "Is the sound system on?"

"Who are you?"

"Samantha Mason. I'm supposed to get the fishermen warmed up for the casting tournament."

"Honey, just looking at you raised the temperature in here ten degrees." He pulled a folded list from inside his uniform. Giving the list a once over, he shook his head. "Your name isn't on the list."

"What? That's impossible." She nudged him lightly in the ribs. "I hope they don't forget to put my name on the paycheck. Flying in here from Dallas and staying at the Hyatt isn't cheap. I'll bet somebody is going to be in big trouble tomorrow."

"Trouble?"

She placed one hand on her hip and fluffed her hair. The whistling behind her increased in volume. "Trouble," Samantha nonchalantly comfirmed. "My name not being on that silly little list will probably cost some typist her job. I just hate that, don't you?"

"Well, I guess it wouldn't hurt anything—"

Samantha grabbed the microphone from his hand. "Thanks!"

Imitating the sexy stride of a Dallas Cowgirl, Samantha strode to the edge of the pool. The number of men on the platform had increased. As she flashed a sunny smile, she clenched her teeth praying that one of those men was the manufacturing representative from a life preserver company. It bothered her to resort to this tactic. She reminded herself of the hours, weeks, months, she'd spent on this project, not to mention the slow dwindling of her cash reserves down to nearly nothing. This was her one big chance. She had to grab it with both hands and run with it.

"Hello Texans!" she boomed into the microphone. "Wait til you see what I have for you lucky fishermen!"

She paused, waiting for the cheering and clapping to end.

"I'm here to introduce the most fantastic, the most revolutionary, the most awesome product ever to hit Texas!"

Samantha turned and froze. On the opposite end of the width of the platform were two security guards headed in her direction. They paused long enough to compare lists with the stage-crew manager she'd spoken to, but now they were bee-lining straight toward her. She didn't have to hear their shouts to know what they were saying.

"Presenting... *Save-A-Man* trunks! Developed and designed by Samantha Ann Mason!" She hustled down the length of the platform, her tongue moving faster than her feet. "Don't know how to swim? Get SAM! Fall from your boat? Get SAM! Want to laze around in fifty feet of water? Get SAM!

"What do you want to get?"

"SAM!" the audience shouted.

"Who can save your life?"

"SAM!"

"Texans, are you going to let a bulky old vest cover up your chest? What do you want instead?"

"SAM!"

"Did I hear Mae West?"

"SAM!"

"See that man. He has on SAM!" Samantha raised both arms shouting, "He'd drown without them!"

The word drown had barely passed between her lips when Jack executed a splashless dive into the pool. Samantha groaned inwardly. Anyone who couldn't swim sure as hell couldn't dive.

With the security men seconds away, she blared, "I can't swim! But I have on..." She tossed the microphone toward the guards and jumped into the pool.

Millions of bubbled blocked the reverberating "SAM!" from reaching her ears. The water closing over her head panicked her. Eyes squeezed shut, she plunged downward, going deeper and deeper.

*Where's the bottom!* Certain she'd descended fathoms, she began to struggle. She'd tested the swimsuit. It worked in shoulder-deep water! Why wasn't it working now?

She swallowed the air in her puffed-out cheeks, certain it was her last. The epitaph that would grace her tombstone in front of her eyes: *Samantha Mason, inventor extraordinaire, wearing her latest invention, drowned while thousands watched.*

"Jack!" she bubbled soundlessly. She felt something claw at her below her rib cage. Scared beyond rational thought, her eyelids sprang open. *Sharks!*

She kicked backward to ward off the attack. Her toe landed against solid bone, but the predator tenaciously wrapped his arms around her waist. *Sharks don't have arms,* was her last coherent thought as the monster's teeth tangled in her hair.

Seconds later, her face broke the surface of the tank. What had been less than half a minute, seemed like hours.

Samantha coughed as she gulped air. Her lungs felt as though they were on fire. She could hear voices chanting, "SAM! SAM! SAM!"

"You okay? Straighten your arms out. Spread your feet! Dammit, those people think they paid to see this stunt!"

Hearing a real live human voice, Samantha lunged toward it. "Oh my God," she babbled, stringing the words into what sounded like one word. "You aren't a shark-octopus-monster! You saved me!"

She opened her eyes to the most welcome sight in the world—Jack Martin.

Jack grinned. The crowd roared, cheering them.

"Kiss 'er! Kiss 'er!"

"Oh, what the hell," he muttered, forgetting everything but the warm woman clinging to him. "They ought to get something for their money." And with that, Jack lowered his mouth to her parted lips.

# Two

What are you so flaming mad about? You should be thanking your lucky stars that the security guards helped us from the pool. We could have been arrested," Jack growled, tossing her pink jogging suit to her. "Didn't I do everything you asked?"

Sam glared at him and sniffed. She could still taste the chlorine from the tank. "Did I ask you to *dive* into the pool?"

"Did you ask me whether or not I could swim? I didn't realize 'jump into the pool' meant—"

"*Jump into the pool* is pretty explicit, isn't it? And I sure as shooting didn't tell you to swim!"

"You didn't tell me not to."

"Ned said you couldn't!"

"Well, Ned stretches the facts about a lot of things."

"He didn't stretch the facts this time. He specifically said that you did not swim." Sam brushed damp curls back from her face.

"So build a scaffold and hang me! Ned lied, and I'm supposed to be punished? Not very logical, my dear."

"Don't you 'my dear' me," she huffed. Employees weren't supposed to lie. And anyone with a lick of sense knew that if the employee did lie, then the boss was supposed to swear to the lie! "Ned works for you. You should have backed him up by floundering in the pool."

She grabbed the pants of her sweat suit and yanked them over the wet bottom of her swimsuit. From the twinkle in Jack's expressive dark eyes, Samantha knew he considered her logic convoluted. "I hear that laughter bottled up in your chest."

"Any other major crimes I committed?" Jack teased her.

"The worst! Did I ask you to kiss me in front of a roaring crowd?"

Jack tossed his head back and roared. "Now that is unforgivable. Bring on the lynch mob. But for heaven's sake, lower your voice. You're starting to draw the crowd away from the main event at the pool."

"*And* you scared the holy livin' daylights out of me. I wasn't mistaken about one thing. A monster did have me by the hair. You!"

"Shhhhh!" Jack dropped his voice to a whisper. "Now you listen to me, you little spitfire. I probably saved your life. I have a bruise on my thigh to prove it."

"Ha! You ruined the whole presentation. The applause was for the kiss, not the trunks."

"Shhhhh! I can't believe you conned me into doing something I knew was so damned foolish. You should have heard what one of those women up there called me. *Beefcake!*"

Samantha's lips twitched, then curved into a smile. "That's a compliment, not an insult. It means—"

"I'm aware of what it means. The description hardly fits my self-image."

Cocking her head to one side, Samantha slowly eyed him from rakish black hair to bluntly cut toenails. "Beefcake. Definitely, my vote agrees with hers."

"Sounds like an item on a women's libber's menu," Jack grumbled. "But, speaking of beef and cake, reminds me, you owe me a dinner."

"You welshed on your end of the bargain. I'm not taking any kissing swimmer to dinner. Give me the trunks you're wearing and we'll call it even."

"Like hell. Take me to dinner. Then I'll give you the trunks," he countered.

"You give me those trunks or I'll get a cop over here to arrest you for theft."

Jack wiped his face on his handkerchief. While they'd been talking, he'd pulled his slacks on over the trunks, and was now buttoning his shirt. His skin crawled as the shirt stuck to his damp chest. He could feel rivulets of water dripping from the trunks' fabric, ruining his expensive slacks. His determination not to let Samantha out of his sight warred with his meticulous nature.

"Come and get them," he challenged.

Samantha smiled sweetly and picked up the gauntlet. "How would you like for the beefcake admirer to remove them? I'm certain that can be arranged easily."

"Welsher. This tiff we're having is because you don't want to live up to your end of the agreement. I've heard about you inventors," he goaded her.

"I'm not like other inventors. I admit to borrowing from my friends and relatives, but I pay them back one way or another."

"You owe me a dinner. Pay up."

"You just follow in my footsteps, Jack Martin. I'm going to fix you a doozy of a dinner!" And with that declaration of war, she wheeled around and marched toward the exit and out to the parking lot. "My car is over there in row DD. Where's yours?"

"I'll ride with you."

"You're going to leave your car here?" she asked, stunned. Leaving a car in a parking lot in Houston was sheer folly. By morning it would be towed away or stolen. "You're inviting disaster."

"I've had my quota of disasters for the day, thank you." Jack let her lead the way. Her soaked sneakers squished as she walked, leaving wet footprints. "Speaking of disasters, did you know that lightning strikes someone more often than an inventor sells a patent?"

"I've heard a similar statistic. The odds for winning the Irish Sweepstakes are better, too." Samantha lifted her shoulders and spread her hands. "It's what I am."

"You sound as though you didn't have any choice in the matter."

Samantha's lips pressed together in a straight line. She'd tried to explain to other men exactly what being an inventor entailed and failed. Her own parents couldn't understand why she wasn't like other normal, attractive women. At her age, she should have a doting husband, two point five kids, a nice suburban home and a station wagon in the driveway. What's good enough for mother ought to be good enough for daughter. The men she'd dated had the same opinion. The thought of being 'normal' made Sam shiver.

"I didn't. But I don't expect you to understand. Few people do."

"Try me."

Unexpectedly, she turned and stopped. Jack bumped against her and caught her shoulders to keep from knocking her down. Light from a nearby streetlight flooded her upturned face.

"Why?"

"Why not?" he countered, stroking the slight hollow near her neck with his thumb. Beneath her jogging suit he could feel the warmth of her skin. The dim light in the parking lot made her facial features an alluring study of planes and hollows. Samantha Mason was one of the most beautiful women he'd met.

"Because..." Samantha tried to back away from him, but something undefinable in his eyes and the way he lightly held her made her heart accelerate. "It won't work. We'd both be wasting our time."

"I'm attracted to you," he murmured. "What about you?"

Samantha's protective instincts made her want to deny the attraction. She'd learned from the trial-and-fail method exactly what to expect: First mutual physical attraction, then several enjoyable dates, quickly followed by the man's ego being pricked when she was late or totally forgot about him when she was working on a new project. The attraction would dwindle in direct proportion to the male ego being deflated. Then, the end would come with both of them being disappointed and hurt.

She placed her hand on the front of his damp shirt, intending to break contact with him. Her hand lingered, exploring the small nub beneath the thin fabric.

"Don't be misled by the packaging. I'm not the kind of woman you'd be interested in. Believe me, I know. Let me pay my debt without emotional complications."

"You're avoiding the question. Are you attracted to me?"

His finger slid beneath her chin, keeping her from ducking the question and prevaricating with her answer.

"Yes. But I've been attracted to other men. It never works. It won't work with you."

Jack lifted her chin a fraction of an inch higher. He read the shadows of pain darkening her eyes. The compelling urge to protect her, to change the course of her life, surprised him. Those sorts of impulses led to the church altar. Confirmed bachelors of thirty-two avoided them.

For a second he wished Ned had made an arrangement with Samantha for a evening of pleasure. He wanted her. But for some reason he couldn't understand, he wanted more than a fleeting interlude.

Back off, he silently warned himself while, at the same time, wrapping his arms around her shoulders. His mind told him to push her away, but another stronger, compelling force told him to draw her closer.

"You're making a big mistake," Samantha cautioned him, voicing his thoughts.

"I'll do a risk-factor analysis in the morning. Right now, with you in my arms, I'm not thinking too clearly."

"Trust me. You won't be courting a woman. You'll be courting a disaster. My nickname isn't Serendipity Sam for nothing. Everyone knows I'm an accident walking around looking for a place to happen."

Jack hugged her. "I survived the first accident."

"You mean diving into the tank?"

"Uh-huh." Jack chuckled. "I survived being in over my head and managed to save you at the same time. Maybe that was symbolic of our future." He kept one arm around her shoulder and turned her toward her car. "Incidentally, serendipity doesn't mean accident-prone. Serendipity is the art of making fortunate discoveries unexpectedly."

Gnawing her lower lip thoughtfully, Sam felt herself going under for the third time. Somehow she had to change his definition back to the one she'd intended when she'd first mentioned it to him.

"That's my VW over there." Samantha watched for his reaction. Only the roof wasn't dented or scraped. The front bumper was buckled in the middle. "Serendipity Sam found a couple of places to have accidents."

"Is that a subtle way of telling me you're high risk in more ways than your insurance premium?"

"Yeah. If it wasn't for the state of Texas requiring insurance, hence requiring the insurance companies to cover high-risk people like me, I'd have been canceled out years ago."

"Okay, Samantha. You've made your point. I'm risking my life just riding with you." He grinned as he opened her unlocked door. "I'll buckle up."

Samantha rummaged through the plastic bag that dangled from her wrist, searching for the keys to the car. They have to be here, she thought. She had to have had them to have gotten to Astro Hall. Why couldn't the car be voice activated? Or instead of a key, why couldn't the owner's thumbprint pressed against the dashboard start the engine? Her hand stilled as her mind swirled with the possibility.

"Samantha?" Jack slammed the passenger door. She was staring through the windshield, holding her breath. "Sam? Is something wrong?"

Sam didn't hear him. Dad would be able to help me, she thought. No one knew the intricate workings of a car better than Pasadena's best automobile mechanic.

*"Sam!"* Jack touched her sleeve. Her head jerked up as though he'd touched her with a cattle prod. "Your keys are in the ignition."

"Oh," she responded vaguely, wondering if an electrical ignition system could be replaced with a heat sensor.

"Earth to Serendipity Sam. Come in," Jack teased, noting the vague, spacy look in her eyes. He leaned forward and brushed his lips against hers.

"Oh! Jack!" She blinked to clear the image of an ignition system she'd seen in one of her father's automobile manuals from her mind. "Keys. I'm looking for my keys."

"They're dangling from the steering column. Lady, you need a keeper. Someone could have stolen your car while you were in there convincing me to—"

Samantha cut the soft-spoken tirade with laughter. "Who'd be dumb enough to steal Sassy?"

"Sassy? You named your car Sassy?"

She twisted the key, and the VW coughed, sputtered, then backfired twice.

"Can you think of a more appropriate name? Make her work when she'd rather be parked and she'll sass you until you stop. Won't you, Sassy?" Samantha shifted gears. Sassy protested with a grinding noise and a loud pop. The car shuddered, rattled, then lunged forward, its tires screeching. Raising her voice over the clatter, Sam yelled, "That a girl."

Perched like a bullfrog on a lily pad, Jack held on for dear life. Trying to carry on a conversation was impossible. After five minutes of Sassy's loud muffler system, Jack was fervently wishing he'd insisted on driving his late-model sedan. Going down the highway on a skateboard had to be safer than this.

Sam grinned, punching the accelerator with her foot once they'd gone through the parking lot gate. "Little old lady in Pasadena sold Sassy to me. Pasadena, Texas, that is. Guess the Texas variety of little old ladies came west in a buckboard?"

With his teeth jarring together dangerously, Jack dared not reply. His head bobbed up and down as Sam hit every pothole with unerring accuracy.

Twenty torture-filled minutes later, Sam careened into a strip shopping center, announcing, "We're here."

Jack opened his eyes and looked around. "Where?"

"Home, but don't tell the owners of the shopping center. The lease forbids living in the shop."

"A home-cooked meal?" Jack asked hopefully, jerking on the door handle, anxious to get as far away from Sassy as quickly as he possibly could.

"More or less. Sit tight, I'll get your door. It only opens from outside." Samantha patted the dashboard. "Thanks, Sassy. Another adventure in driving successfully accomplished."

Doubts began to flicker in Jack's mind. What was he doing with a woman like Samantha? His taste generally ran toward sleek, sophisticated women who didn't talk to their cars, who didn't talk him into jumping into pools of water and who didn't drive like maniacs or live in shopping centers.

Opening his door, Samantha watched Jack uncurl himself, and smiled with satisfaction at the expression on his face. Somewhere between Astro Hall and Pasadena, she'd discovered she sincerely liked Jack. The kindest thing she could do would be to let him see for himself how different they were. Between Sassy and her shop, she predicted that within ten minutes he'd be running into the street without looking back.

"Need some help getting out? Sassy takes some getting used to."

Jack took the hand she offered. "Next time, we'll take my car. That your dress shop?" he asked once his feet were on firm ground.

Sam laughed. "Don't you wish. Mine is next door. Sam's Fixit Shop."

"Maybe after I've eaten you could fix my back," Jack said, putting his hands on his hips and arching his shoulders backward. "I think it's broken."

"Complaining already? Maybe you'd like to skip dinner. I'll call a cab."

"No way, Samantha. I was just looking for an excuse to have you massage my back." He winked, casting her a lopsided grin. "You aren't going to get rid of me that easily."

From two stores down, Samantha heard Melissa Parker calling her. "Yoo-hoo! Sam!"

Melissa ran a drapery shop to support herself until Hollywood discovered the new Marilyn Monroe was alive, well and earning a living in Pasadena.

Unaware of what she was doing, Samantha tightened her grip on Jack's hand. When Jack returned the slight squeeze, she instantly dropped his hand.

What's wrong with me? Sam silently quizzed herself. I should be pushing him in Melissa's direction!

"Well, well, well," Melissa crooned, her eyes running the length and breadth of Jack, "what have we here?"

"Melissa Parker, meet Jack Martin."

Fluttering her inch-long lashes, Melissa asked, "Where did you find him?'

"At the bottom of a fishing tank," Jack answered, taking the hand Melissa offered. "It's nice to meet you."

"My pleasure, I'm certain," Melissa whispered in her best Marilyn Monroe imitation. Her wide blue eyes glanced between Jack and Samantha on a direct course to the flower shop behind them. A tall male figure cast a shadow on the window. Samantha Mason wasn't the only woman furious with Jacob Klein.

"Are you on your way to dinner? I owe Jack a dinner, but I'm certain he'd rather—"

"Welsher," Jack muttered loudly enough for Samantha to hear, but not Melissa.

"Oh, Sam, I'd just love to eat with Jack, but I'm on my way to an audition."

"Isn't it kind of late?" Sam blurted. Many a morning she'd covered for Melissa at the drapery shop while she auditioned for various parts in local plays. Any part Melissa would be auditioning for at nine o'clock at night wouldn't be allowed in a legitimate theater.

A smile like the cat who swallowed the canary lit Melissa's face. "You wouldn't believe who came in the shop today. A producer! He's giving me a private reading."

Sam groaned aloud. "That's the oldest line in the book!"

"Not this time. He had a printed business card. He's the real McCoy."

"Anyone can have a card printed." She nudged Jack forward. "Do you know anybody in show business, Jack?"

"I haven't been to a movie in years, much less a play." The harder Samantha pushed, the more he dug his heels in. "Nice meeting you, Melissa. We won't keep you any longer."

"Oh, honey, if I didn't have a producer waiting, you and I could produce a smash hit," Melissa flirted, walking her fingers up his chest. She hoped the florist's hazel eyes were turning pea green with jealousy. "Another time?"

"No time like the present," Samantha protested, feeling Jack's biceps flex beneath her hand.

"Do you have something for me?" Melissa asked Sam in her normal squeaky voice.

"Not yet." Samantha felt her cheeks turning red. "I'm working on it."

"I can't pass the test unless you . . ."

"You're going to be late." Sam could see curiosity written all over Jack's face.

"You've had the drapes for two months," Melissa pouted. "You promised you'd invent something."

"Soon," Sam promised.

"Terrific! Ciao!" Melissa said, waving and making certain she stepped on the hot-air duct as she strutted down the sidewalk. Predictably, her light-weight circular skirt fluttered to her waist.

Jack groaned aloud.

"She's a nice girl. Star struck but nice."

Samantha unlocked the shop door, flipped the light switch, went in and pulled the drapes. The managers of the adjoining stores turned a blind eye to her living there, but Ralph Jenkins, who managed the chain supermarket, wouldn't approve of her entertaining a man in her shop.

Thinking of Ralph reminded Sam that she had to fix his kids' broken toys before Monday. There weren't enough hours in the day to accommodate working on her latest project, marketing SAM trunks, and to fix toys and appliances to keep a roof over her head and food on the table.

She certainly didn't have time for Jack Martin.

"Interesting place you have here," Jack said diplomatically.

"You mean cluttered and disorganized, don't you?"

"Interesting," he reiterated. Make-do shelves and tables haphazardly stacked with everything from small appliances to toys crowded the entire room. "You must be some sort of mechanical genius to take this stuff apart and put it back together again."

"The mechanical genius is the person who invented it, not the person who repairs it," she corrected. Striding to the cash register, she rang the No Sale key. Sam handed him a wrinkled five-dollar bill. "There's a Burger-doodle on the corner. Hamburger, fries and a milk shake? This should take care of my debt."

Jack stuck his hands in his slacks pockets. The damp inner lining, warm from his flesh, reminded him of the excuse he needed to politely refuse. "Aren't you forgetting? I have something that belongs to you."

Afraid his staying would result in him taking something far more important than the prototype of her invention, Sam slowly closed the till. "Take the money. Melissa..."

"I'm not interested in Melissa's charms."

"For Pete's sake, look around you." Her arm made an arc around the walls of the shop.

"I am looking, and I like what I see."

"The back room, where I live, is worse," she warned. "What can I do to convince you to leave?"

He appeared to ponder the question seriously. The twinkle in his dark, mischievous eyes warned Samantha before he spoke. Jack sauntered toward the counter.

"You could shave those impudent golden locks of yours that my fingers are itching to twine through. A gunnysack would hide those very lush curves of yours. Maybe a paper sack over your head—"

"Don't touch anything," she squeaked when his forearm raked the small pieces of a fishing reel aside. "I won't be able to get it back together again if pieces are missing."

"That's what you're worried about, isn't it? Not being able to put the pieces back together again if I stay?"

All pretense at humoring her evaporated as he reached across the counter and lightly held her shoulders. Her lower lip trembled with uncertainty. His warm breath fanned her face, sending shivers down her spine.

"Some things can't be fixed," she said, her voice shaking.

Samantha knew about heartbreak. Each time her heart shattered with disappointment, she promised herself never again. Like a gambler who faithfully vows not to touch a deck of cards again, she knew her weaknesses. And she knew her inventive mind led to emotional bankruptcy with the same certainty a gambler knows the odds are with the house. Samantha had learned from experience that good luck and romantic dreams came with limited guarantees. Better to fold the hand and walk away none the richer than to gamble with love.

Samantha closed her eyes and withdrew from his loose hold. "I'll fix dinner."

Jack watched her push aside the drawn curtain covering the doorway to the back room. He sensed her vulnerability. Underneath the gutsy woman who'd nearly drowned herself to prove her invention lay a fragile child-woman who'd been wounded. Nothing he could say would reassure her. He'd have to rebuild her confidence in herself as a woman.

"It's ready." Samantha slapped the grape-jelly-covered piece of bread on top of the slice covered with peanut butter. She considered rummaging through the overhead cabinets for a package of potato chips, but decided against it since she couldn't remember when Ralph had brought them to the shop. A P.B. and J. sandwich on day-old bread should be enough to discourage Jack, she thought, plunking it down onto a chipped saucer.

She scooted a stack of mechanical drawings aside and set the sandwich on the small table in one corner. She made a place for him to sit by unloading the newspapers from a metal chair. As he entered the doorway, she folded the sofa bed back into place. Tapping her lip with her finger, she tried to remember where she'd put the cushions.

"How long have you lived here?" Jack asked, comparing the clutter in the shop to the clutter in her living quarters. There wasn't a smidgen of difference between the two.

Snapping her fingers, Samantha dropped to her knees. With a triumphant smile on her face, she pulled two cushions from under the sofa. Living in a room the size of a large bathroom required ingenuity.

"Six months. I had a condo that I bought with the royalties from one invention, but I had a temporary cash-flow problem while I was working on the trunks, so I rented it." She gestured toward the rejection letters used as wallpaper to cover the space over the table. "I've got lots of things circulating. Who knows. Maybe somebody at Astro Hall will be interested in the swimming trunks."

"Have you ever considered working as a research scientist and doing your own thing on the side?" O'Toole Life Preservers, the company he worked for, had such an opening. With his recommendation she might have a chance of getting it.

Sam shoved the cushions into place and rose to her feet. "Only in moments of darkest despair. The thought of a company taking credit for my invention makes this place a palace to me."

"Not a slave to wages, huh?"

"Exactly. I'm not about to be a creative bird caught in a corporate net. Caged birds rarely sing, or in my case, invent. Nobody is going to clip my wings and coop me up in a sterile laboratory. Since you're an expert on lightning striking," she said, referring to Jack's remark about the odds against licensing an invention, "are you aware that only twelve out of seventy-two outstanding inventions since 1889 have been produced by corporation research?''

Jack picked up the sandwich, examined it, then cautiously nibbled the corner. Deciding it was safe, he took a larger bite as he scanned the collage of letters on the wall.

''I'll bet O'Toole's has a ten-foot fence surrounding it, doesn't it?'' she asked, determined to point out metaphorically the difficulties of an inventor getting into the building no less the impossibility of them being able to climb the corporate ladder.

Nodding his head, Jack spied a familiar letterhead: O'Toole Life Preservers, Inc. The gooey peanut butter clogged his throat when he saw his signature at the bottom of the form letter. Samantha was taking potshots at his company, and now he understood why. He'd formally rejected her trunks.

He searched his mind, trying to remember the circumstances. His responsibilities at O'Toole included rubber-stamping the decisions of the technical supervisor, Ted Langston. As though he'd picked the lock on a long-forgotten closed door, the memory of Ted laughing about a zany idea to revolutionize the life jacket industry, squeezed through. The proposed idea, obviously Samantha's, had been sealed in a perfumed envelope marked 'Personal.'

''The fence is there to keep the loonies who work there inside, not to keep the sane people out.'' Samantha watched as the blood seemed to drain from his face. Aware she'd taken a jab at his job and career, she jumped to her feet, ready to apologize.

Jack put his sandwich back on the saucer. His tongue stuck to the roof of his mouth, but he'd managed to swallow. He removed the tape holding the rejection letter to the wall. Much as he wanted to destroy the evidence that would give Samantha the excuse she'd been looking for to kick him out the front door, he handed the damning letter to her.

"I'm Jonathan Martin."

# Three

―――

Samantha glanced from the signature to Jack's face. Taking the letter from his hand, she smoothed the tape, testing it for tackiness, then slapped it back on the wall.

"Well, Jonathan 'Jack' Martin, your letter proved my point. O'Toole had the opportunity to lease the rights to SAM trunks and blew it. Definite lack of foresight on your part, wouldn't you agree?"

She didn't realize how close Jack was until her arm brushed against his chest as the tape refused to stick to the wall. There weren't any ten-foot high fences between them, though heaven knew, she wished there were.

"You're still wet," she stammered. She hastily dropped her hand to her side. The back of her hand tingled with awareness. Automatically her eyes tracked down his chest to the dark trace of water outlining her invention.

She had to get the trunks. The patent on the bonded fabric was pending. She'd had one million-dollar invention stolen. Jack Martin could blithely walk out of here and invent around her idea without paying one red cent for the privilege. Her stomach twisted in a knot tighter than the drawstring in the waistband of SAM trunks.

"Take your pants off and give me—"

Jack grinned. "You're too late to seduce me," he teased, fully aware she wasn't propositioning him. "There's a standard procedure for seduction, just as there is a standard procedure for presenting an invention. I'll admit though, your chlorine fragrance is far more enticing than the perfumed note you sent to Ted."

"Sometimes inventors have to be devious," she said, excusing her method of insuring her letters were opened. "Finish eating your sandwich and give me my trunks."

"Maybe Melissa's producer and I have something in common," he continued, his words half serious, half in jest. "It isn't every day I have an attractive woman demanding that I remove my pants. Of course, I should have been suspicious of your intentions when you insisted I undress in front of you."

Samantha's eyes rounded at the interpretation he was putting on the situation. "Believe me, seducing you is the furtherest thing from my mind."

"You didn't seem shocked when you discovered I was the person who signed that letter. Could it be you knew all along?"

"You know better! I thought you were a sales manager or something."

"Mmmmm. Likely story," Jack said, which brought a pink tinge to her cheeks. "I'm trying to remember—

when you had that death grip on my shoulders, did I kiss you or did you kiss me?''

"You kissed me!" The red tide of embarrassment winged to her widow's peak.

Jack skied his finger down her nose. "You're right, that was my bright idea. What confuses me is, assuming you did know who I was, why did you pretend to be drowning?''

"I wasn't pretending!"

"Oh. You were drowning?"

"Yes!"

"Guess your invention doesn't work then, huh? And since you aren't interested in watching me undress again, I'll just wear these home.''

Samantha moved to the open curtain to block him from leaving. "You aren't going anywhere!"

The pounding on the window of the shop startled her. Ralph Jenkins stood outside the door, holding a sack of groceries in one arm, while he continued to beat on the glass.

"Coming, Ralph!" She swung back toward Jack with one finger over her lips, indicating for him to be quiet. Worried that, while she was in front of the shop talking to Ralph, Mr. Jonathan Martin would snoop around and discover her other projects, she added for good measure, "Don't touch anything. I'm working on something explosive!"

Sam caught his quick nod, then fled to the front door.

"Here," she said, opening the door and extending her arms, "I'll take those groceries. Thanks."

"Is the boat fixed?" Ralph maintained possession of the groceries and entered the shop.

"Let me take those and I'll get it for you." Ralph stubbornly refused to give her the sack. His habit of wandering around the shop with his final destination being the back room, where he usually unloaded the sack and put away the refrigerated goods had Sam's ears pounding. "I'll put them away."

"That my boat over there?" Ralph asked, moving beyond her reach. "My wife said not to keep furnishing you with groceries unless I brought the boat home."

"Ralph, I apologize for not getting it repaired sooner."

"What was wrong with it?"

"Corroded wires from the battery to the propeller. I replaced them with plastic-coated wires. I can't imagine why the manufacturers of remote control boats don't use that kind of wire. They know the kids are going to put the toy in the water." She popped the top part of the boat open for Ralph's inspection. He didn't have the foggiest notion what he was looking at, but he wiggled the battery as though he thoroughly understood mechanical problems.

Samantha glanced over her shoulder. Behind her back, she waved at the finger and eyeball protruding from behind the curtain.

"What about the doll?"

"Your daughter fed it spinach. It blocked up the tube."

"Disgusting. Why my wife bought a diaper doll I'll never understand. She certainly didn't want to change Patty's diapers!"

"I had to order a new tube from the doll company. It should be here in a couple of weeks."

"What about the blender? Did the thingamajig arrive?"

"Oh, yes!"

Samantha stepped behind the counter and retrieved the blender. "Good as new."

"I don't know what I'd do without you, Sam." He reached into the sack and pulled out the bill from the supermarket. His thumb on the bottom figure, he asked, "Are we even?"

"Looks fair to me."

"Jacob added a roast to pay for the electrical display you wired at the floral shop. Is he here?"

"Jacob?" Sam asked, stationing herself between the drape and the grocer.

Ralph poked his wire-framed glasses up the bridge of his nose. "I figured he'd be down on his knees apologizing for not showing up at the Astro Hall. He was flapping around in a real tizzy when his delivery truck broke down. Of course, any man who plays with flowers ought to flap around."

Samantha could tell Ralph was about to settle in for a nice long gossip session.

"I appreciate you bringing the groceries by the shop. I'll drop the doll off at the store as soon as the tube is delivered." With a look that brooked no refusal, she swung the groceries into her arms.

"Now, don't get steamed up. I know Melissa and Jacob are your friends and you won't talk about them behind their backs. Though goodness knows, they're strange."

"Eccentric," Sam substituted, smiling. "I fit right in, don't I?"

Samantha knew Ralph had a few pet theories about her, too. But he excused her strangeness. Inventors weren't supposed to be straight. Everyone, including Ralph, knew that Einstein's socks never matched.

"You're a good girl." He patted her cheek affectionately. "Aren't many girls your age with your high morals. Lax society we live in."

Hearing a strangled noise from behind the curtain, Samantha put her finger under her nose and faked a sneeze.

"You coming down with something?" Ralph inquired, jabbing his glasses. "I thought you looked a bit flushed. Want me to get you some cold syrup from the store before I head home?"

"No! I was cleaning in the back room. Must be the dust."

"It's probably those late hours you've been keeping. You need to go to bed early and stop worrying about making ends meet."

Samantha hooked her empty arm through Ralph's and led him to the door. She tossed a quelling glance over her shoulder. Ralph didn't have any idea that he'd made a double pun, not that the advice he'd given her was exactly opposite to the advice he should have given if she was to remain a 'good girl.'

"Thanks again, Ralph. Don't worry about me. I'll be fine as soon as I clear out the back room." *I hope you're listening, Mr. Big Ears,* Samantha silently added, pasting a polite smile on her face.

Ralph grinned in response. "Got another million-dollar idea you're working on? You didn't tell me how the lifesaving trunks worked."

"They worked."

"Great! Some day I'll be reading about you in the newspaper, and I'll be able to say, 'Without me she'd have starved'."

"And without me, you'd be knee-deep in broken toys."

Ralph nodded as he opened the door. "Lock it. You never know what kind of kook is wandering around the neighborhood."

Wiggling her fingers, Samantha heaved a sigh of relief when Ralph walked to the curb. He stood there, waiting.

Why wasn't he going to his car? She silently cursed. Ralph's wife must be picking him up tonight. She was as notorious for being late as Ralph was for poking his nose into other people's business.

She dashed to the back of the shop, pausing only long enough to grab the groceries. The minute she entered the back room, Jack took the sack and handed her the soggy trunks.

"You can't leave!"

"You're a bundle of contradictions, aren't you? I distinctly recall your rushing me through—" he pointed toward the empty saucer "—dinner."

"The gossip columnist of the shopping center is waiting for his wife out front. You're going to have to stay here until he leaves."

"Sorry about the noise. I tried not to laugh aloud."

"You weren't the only one having difficulty keeping a straight face." Her eyes quickly scanned the room to make certain nothing had been moved. Since her idea for an automatic computer-tape rewinder had been stolen, she hadn't trusted anybody. "Would you mind putting those away for me?"

While Jack unloaded the sack, Samantha nonchalantly spread newspapers over everything on the counters.

"Bartering seems to be a way of life for you," Jack commented. He opened the apartment-size refrigerator under the counter she'd pointed toward. Unable to resist teasing her, he added with faked thoughtfulness, "Now what do I have that you'd be interested in bartering?"

"Nothing."

"Surely you can think of something you need. Companionship? A shoulder to cry on?" He put the last of the groceries away, then rose to his feet. His eyes swept over her as she leaned against the edge of a wide table, one leg extended, toe pointed, and the other foot precariously balanced on a wooden box. "Someone to dust your shelves?"

"Men are more trouble than they're worth," she uttered in a final bid to free herself of Jack's persistence.

"Lady Sam, didn't your mother teach you that men find the unobtainable a challenge?"

Butterflies invaded her stomach when he turned her around and looped her arms around his neck. Being on the box elevated her height. Her defenses weakened. With one last effort she said, "Ralph is gone by now. You can leave."

"Is that what you really want?"

Samantha curbed her tongue. His mention of her mother, a moment ago, had brought to mind all the things her parents had wanted for her. Their top priority centered around a steady man who could make her abandon her bizarre life-style. Jack Martin would be welcomed with open arms.

But what her parents wanted and what she wanted didn't mesh.

Sam, the inventor, wasn't going to set herself up for failure.

"Yes." *No!* her traitorous body refuted stubbornly.

She expected him to release her, to give up on her as a lost cause. His drawing her closer into his arms as though she were a cherished prize made her knees weak. They threatened to buckle when he softly whispered, "Inventors often discover things they aren't searching for. You're no exception."

He teased the valley of her sealed lips with the tip of his tongue. "I'll call . . . soon" was his parting promise.

Her fingers touched the lips he'd barely grazed. His name hummed in her mind as he strode out the front door. Disoriented, Samantha stumbled off the box.

Dammit, Jack Martin—or any other man for that matter—wasn't going to complicate her life.

"I'm happy with the way things are," she muttered, feeling sadly deflated. To lift her spirits, she added more firmly, "I am."

Although she stated her belief with emphatic force, it didn't ring true. She had to convince herself that her beliefs hadn't changed. She began by listing what Jack would do if he became a part of her life.

He'd muck around the shop straightening the clutter, demanding attention, trying to change me, she thought. He's just like any other man. Maybe a bit taller, a tad wittier, a tiny bit smarter, but he's still a man!

Samantha flopped down on the couch, closing her eyes, remembering, allowing the shadows of other men to rise from the recesses of her mind. She needed to refresh her memory in order to repair the damage Jack Martin had inflicted.

Looking back, she didn't know if she'd ever been in love. The idea of being in love had appealed to her. But like many of her inventions, love simply wasn't feasible.

Had it always been that way? Had she always been such a misfit?

Until her teenage years, the boys thought she was great. She fixed their toys, roughhoused, and climbed trees with them. Her best friends were boys, not dolls or giggly girls.

When had her relationship with boys changed? Sam knew.

Puberty! The age when funloving boys turn into raunchy, pint-sized men.

Samantha hated the way her body had changed. She'd liked being a skinny, long-legged tomboy who could race with the wind and win. Mother Nature didn't give her a choice.

By the time she was thirteen, the boys were more interested in watching her T-shirt slide to her shoulders as she hung by her knees than in trying to copy her trick. Much as she tried to ignore their sniggers, she gave up outdoing them on the playground bars.

And then, at fourteen, the inevitable happened. She developed a tremendous crush on a neighborhood boy, Bob Cranson. Sam was competitive by nature and Bob was the only boy who could beat her at every sport without it bothering her. Bob hung the moon and set the stars in place—a perfect setting for her romantic dreams.

To her dismay, she wasn't the only girl who had noticed Bob. Compounding her dismay was the fact that the girls weren't the only ones noticing how the opposite sex had changed. Bob flirted with anything in tight jeans or a skirt. He wasn't particular.

Sam decided she'd get his sole attention by creating something spectacular and giving it to him, something special, something no other girl could make. She brainstormed for weeks, searching for an idea that would dazzle him.

One day, as she watched him pedal by her house on his new Pro Classic ten-speed, lightning struck. She knew Bob was proud of his bicycle, but what he *really* wanted was a Harley Davidson motorcycle. With that thought in mind, Sam cleverly dissected what made the motorcycle so appealing. Could a bike be converted? She toyed with the idea of tearing her dad's lawn-mower apart and mounting the motor on the bike but decided Bob's love wasn't worth mowing the yard with a push mower. Finally, electricity crackling in her mind, she had the answer.

She'd make Bob's bike *sound* like a Harley David-son.

Once she'd designed, tested and perfected the noise-maker, she asked Bob to drop by her house after school. With a shy smile, she promised to give him something better than any other girl could give him.

Samantha could practically hear her innocent re-mark. The advantages of age and hindsight now en-abled her to understand why Bob had expected something other than a noisemaker. But at the time, she thought her gift an awesome present.

She smiled, remembering how her heart fluttered the moment his kickstand touched the pavement of her driveway. Within seconds, she began dismantling his rear wheel. No amount of protesting on his part could stop her greasy little hands. When he grabbed her, pulling her against his chest, as his lips descended, the oil can in her hand squirted its contents across his shirt, cheeks and nose.

Right then, Samantha mused, I should have known love and inventors don't mix. The rascal didn't even wave as he loudly sped out of sight.

Her other attempts at being in love had met similar fates. She recalled almost electrocuting poor Mike. Of course, she thought, justifying herself, he should have known better than to stand in a puddle of water while she plugged in the prototype of a miniature windmill. If she could have bottled the energy he used when he screamed, yelled and beat his chest, she could have solved the nation's energy crisis without the windmill.

And then there was Andrew the photographer. A broken date ruined that romance. She'd tried to explain. He'd refused to listen to reason. Why hadn't Andrew been able to get it into his thick skull that he'd caused her to forget their date? She remembered she'd started to get dressed and her zipper had stuck. She'd reached over her shoulder but hadn't been able to reach the zipper. Then she'd tried the opposite direction. But the zipper had been caught dead center in the middle of her back. That was when inspiration struck. Every woman needed a zipper unsticker. So what if she'd been a few hours late? She'd apologized. She'd gone the extra mile by offering to fix his broken wide-angle camera lens. Nothing appeased him. In fact, he'd insulted her by saying she'd probably lose his expensive lens in that mess she called a shop.

And last but not least was Tom the thief: the computer genius who had an idea but not the mechanical aptitude to make drawings or to design prototypes. Sam had thought he wanted to steal her heart, but what Tom stole was her virginity and the automatic rewinder for computer tapes. The sad part, from Sam's viewpoint, was that she would have given him the designs as wholeheartedly as she'd given herself. But Tom had wanted more. He'd wanted complete credit and the profits derived from the invention.

Heartsick, Sam had realized she'd failed as a woman.

It was after Tom left that she set her priorities in order. Men were at the bottom of the list. Creative juices and sex drive were incompatible. She had faith in her inventions. Someday one of her million-dollar ideas would make her rich, rich, rich. And when that day arrived, she wouldn't share the credit with any man.

Sam let her eyes drift around the room. Organized confusion, she thought, rationalizing the clutter. She knew exactly where every nut, bolt and spring was located. So what if a stranger couldn't find anything. Strangers didn't work here. It wasn't their problem.

Her eyes lingered on the Turn Out the Lights invention she'd covered with newspapers. This invention and Jack Martin had a lot in common. She could get the lights on, but she couldn't turn them off with a wave of her finger. From Jack's departing words, she was certain he wasn't easily turned off either.

"Must have a screw loose," she muttered, standing, putting her hands on her hips. She'd shown him exactly who and what she was. "What more could I have done to dissuade him?"

Jack's thoughts were similar as he tipped the cab driver, and strode into his condominium overlooking Clear Lake. Although Samantha's physical attributes weren't anything to sneeze at, he'd certainly been exposed to equally attractive women.

Exposed? He'd certainly done that! No other woman could have convinced him to undress in the middle of Astro Hall!

He looked down at his slacks and shoes. He wiggled his toes and felt the inner cushion part from the leather. Chalk those up on the deficit side of the column, he thought, automatically visualizing a success versus failure chart in his mind.

On the plus side, he made a note of the SAM trunks. While the security guards had been chasing Samantha, he'd followed her explicit instructions, and to his amazement, the trunks had supported his weight. Panic, he decided, must have been the factor that made them useless for Samantha. Had she followed her own directions, she would have floated to the surface.

Jack grinned as he remembered the way she wrapped her arms and legs around him. On dry land and without the audience, having her in a similar position was something he'd definitely put on the plus side of the chart. The memory of the way she'd returned his kiss certainly balanced the damage to his clothing.

Crossing to the built-in bar, he poured himself a shot of Wild Turkey. He took a sip and savored the fiery sensation on his tongue.

Samantha was a nut, but she knew it. Heavens above, she flaunted it like a warning flag that read: "Don't come near me. I'm hazardous to your health. I don't cook, clean or care to learn. I'm an inventor. Period."

Jack pondered an idea. In jest he'd teased her about knowing who he was ahead of time. But any inventor who sent a perfumed letter to the technical supervisor at O'Toole wasn't above using her feminine powers to convince the plant supervisor to test her invention. And, he thought, what about her tactic of verbally pushing him away while physically pulling him closer? Was it all a clever deception?

Or was she too honest?

Jack respected honesty. He also readily admitted that her life-style, based on the early American tradition of bargaining, couldn't be faulted. Not for her, but what about him?

Fifteen years at O'Toole Life Preserver, Inc., had taught him the value of hard work and monetary reward. When he'd said that he'd set up an interview with his company, she'd flatly refused. Money wasn't important to her.

The thought of Samantha spinning her wheels, getting nowhere, inventing things for the pure pleasure of knowing she could make an idea work horrified Jack. He'd told her there was a proper procedure for everything and he'd meant it.

Samantha Mason, from perfumed letter to Astro Hall demonstration, had violated every procedure for getting a product licensed. His quick glance at Ted's rejection letter indicated her distrust toward manufacturers. That Ted had rejected SAM trunks was no surprise to Jack.

Why didn't inventors realize a technical supervisor was safer if he ignored all novelties from the outside?

If the research supervisor picked a loser, his firm never forgot his poor choice. Should a winner slip through his fingers, by the time it was marketed, management would have forgotten the crackpot who sent the perfumed letter. Multimillion dollar corporations could afford to wait and see, then buy up the new idea when it was proven. Few people grasped the intricacies of making a company sit up and take notice of anything new or different. And even fewer had the inside experience to understand the time, trouble and expense involved in producing an invention of any kind.

Jack seriously doubted that Sam had any concept of cost, overhead, distribution or replacement of damaged merchandise. Profit? Samantha could barter to obtain the necessities of life, but the lady didn't have the vaguest notion of how to make money. To her, those were mundane problems beneath careful consideration.

He thoughtfully sipped his Wild Turkey.

What Samantha needed was a Jonathan Martin in her life. Someone who realized the last place you'd present flotation trunks would be to a manufacturer whose life blood was flotation vests. What did Sam expect? Did she truly believe O'Toole would risk destroying the profit made from the vests to produce the trunks? Why take the chance? What appeared to Sam as the logical place to present her idea was the worst possible choice. Going into competition with oneself was a sure fire way of going out of business. If she had him directing her projects, he'd know the who, where and how of marketing her patents.

With that pleasant prospect lingering in his mind, Jack set his drink on the bar, walked to his bedroom and began to undress. Samantha challenged him personally and professionally. Jonathan 'Jack' Martin wasn't a man who ignored a challenge. He silently bet that within three months he could turn Samantha's life around and get her headed in a more profitable direction.

# Four

Marilyn would have given her left boob to have been in your shoes last night. Who was that gorgeous hunk of a man?" Melissa leaned over the table where Sam was dismantling a toaster.

"Nobody in particular," Sam replied in an offhand manner to dissuade Melissa from pursuing the topic. Throughout the night, she'd pinched herself awake to interrupt her dreams starring Jack Martin. She didn't want to think about him, much less discuss him with Melissa. "How'd the interview with the producer go?"

"It fizzled." Melissa lifted her breasts. "You've got to do something about these!"

"You're paying the price for going braless too many years. The laws of gravity do take their toll."

Melissa placed the back of her hand to her forehead. "Howard Hughes where are you when I need you? He must have made his first fortune off the underwire bra he designed for Jane Russell."

"Where did you read that piece of trivia?"

"In a movie magazine."

Sam groaned her skepticism. "Did this same magazine say your chances of being a star are determined by the shape of your boobies?"

"I'm no dummy. I figured that out by myself," Melissa replied smugly. "I told you about failing the booby test last month. I could have cried when that director had us line up, put our hands behind our head and make our elbows touch the wall. You know who got the part."

"I know. The girl whose boobs touched the wall before her elbows did. I also know the play closed ten minutes after the curtain rose. Be content with what you've got."

"Like you?" Melissa dramatically shuddered. "No thanks. I know making these setters into pointers would make me a Hollywood star. You promised to design something."

"Hand me the tweezers over there by the cash register, would you?"

Melissa flounced across the shop. "Maybe the reason you aren't designing a new bra for me is because you want all the gorgeous hunks to yourself."

"Not likely," Sam muttered, carefully unscrewing a small nut.

"What about last night?" Melissa dropped the tweezers on the table. "Jack what's-his-name didn't look as though he needed anything repaired. I saw the gleam in his eye when he looked at you." Her voice rose with indignation. "Why, he barely noticed me."

"Believe me, you were noticed. How can you accuse me of monopolizing Jack when I tried to get you to go to dinner with him? You're the one who sashayed down the sidewalk too soon."

"Do you really think he liked me?" Melissa moistened the tip of her little finger and ran it over the arch of her eyebrow. "Really?"

"He'd be a fool not to be interested," Samantha said, telling Melissa what she wanted to hear in an effort to end the conversation.

"Maybe you could call him and sort of let him know I don't have a dinner date tonight," Melissa wheedled.

The tiny screw she'd been diligently trying to remove toppled into the burnt leavings in the bottom of the toaster. "Melissa, I'm too busy to call. Think of the poor woman who is having to eat plain bread until I fix her toaster."

"I knew you didn't want to help me," Melissa sniveled. "Think about poor me for a change. This morning I had to lift my boobies before I could buckle my belt."

"You're exaggerating, Melissa. It isn't that bad."

"Yet. That's what you're thinking. I know it is. Next week I'll have to push them aside to pull on my pantyhose!" she wailed.

Samantha jumped to her feet. "Okay! Okay! You win! The toaster can wait. Dry those fake tears and come over here."

"Oooh Sam! I knew I could count on you. Where's the wire you tried last time. Never mind! I see it. It's over there under the broken telephone."

"We're going to try something totally different. I checked out an engineering book on building suspension bridges from the library. Unless I'm mistaken, the same principles of physics apply. What we're going to do is support the weight from point A—" she pointed toward Melissa's left side "—to point B—" she pointed toward Melissa's right side "—using your shoulders as anchors to your superstructure."

"Sounds terrific! If this works, I could change my stage name to something like...Sandy Francisco." Melissa lifted herself up to allow new measurements to be taken. "Do you think Jack would go see me in a movie if that was my name?"

"Will you please stop bobbing up and down? And forget about Jack Whazzisname."

"But Sam," Melissa protested, "I can't help but wonder what you did to make him ignore me. He couldn't get rid of me fast enough. I wonder—"

"Melissa, you're beginning to make me wonder also." She raised the plastic coated wire and looped it around her friend's neck. "Do you think if I stretched your neck several inches it would have the same effect as when you lift your arms? You know, like that famous actress with the long neck?"

"Oh, yeah! But she was flat chested. Is that why? Some crazy inventor stretched her neck and her boobs disappeared." Melissa fluttered her lashes, as though long necks and no boobs made sense to her. Not taking any chances of completely loosing her most valuable asset, she hastily backed out of reach.

Ashamed of herself for alarming Melissa, Sam lowered the wire. "You don't need Jack Martin to make your life complete."

"Women's libber," Melissa scoffed. "Men run this world."

"Your world, not mine."

"You may kid yourself into believing you're different from the rest of us, but the last laugh will be on you.

You're the only person I know who needs a man worse than I do.''

"Wrong."

"Right! Mr. Right!!"

Samantha steadily advanced. Melissa picked up her cue and imitated the lead star in a Stephen King horror film she'd seen. "You keep your car away from me!"

"Sassy?"

"Christine!"

"Who the heck is Christine?" Sam asked, totally perplexed.

"The star in Stephen King's movie. Didn't you see it? Christine was a demented car. She had to pass the boobie test, too!" Melissa giggled as she opened the shop door. "She had great big bumpers!"

Samantha smacked her forehead with the palm of her hand. "I'm convinced. I'll work on the design!"

"Sam? When Mr. Right calls, would you give him my number?" A fresh round of girlish giggles bubbled from Melissa as Sam's phone rang. "It's him!"

"Out! The crazy scientist has to hang up on Mr. Right and then get busy!"

Samantha waited until Melissa had gone before she picked up the phone. "Pasadena Dog Pound," she said, determined to keep Mr. Right from tracking her down.

"Samantha? Is that you?"

"Mother!" Sam glanced at the calendar on the wall to no avail. She'd forgotten to rip off the month of May. "Is it Sunday?"

"No, dear. It's Friday, all day."

"But you usually don't call until Sunday morning."

"I know, dear, but I had this premonition."

"That I wasn't coming to dinner on Sunday?"

Her mother's premonitions had seldom changed over the years since Sam had left home. They were centered around her moving back in with her parents or her being madly in love or her announcing she was going to present them with a grandchild. She strummed her fingers on the counter, patiently waiting for her mother to start her spiel. Sam knew them all by heart.

"Did you know you made the late news last night?"

"I did? Wow! Do you know what that could mean for SAM trunks?"

"SAM trunks? The newscaster didn't say anything about anyone's luggage."

"Remember the fabric I showed you that had the peculiar lining? I had a seamstress make them into swim suits. I named them *Save-A-Man* SAM trunks."

"That's nice, dear. I wonder why the reporter didn't mention them?"

"He didn't? What did he say?"

"You were in the 'Love in the Strangest Places' segment of the news." Maxine paused. "Your father wants you to bring the young man you were kissing home to meet us."

"I wasn't actually kissing him, Mother."

"Don't invent some story to hide the truth. My eyes may be ancient, but I can tell when my little girl is kissing someone. I told everyone who called this morning that I'd get back to them on Monday and give them a full report."

"Mother! Please don't say anything to anyone. It's a mistake. I don't know the man."

"You don't know him? You must know him! Why were you kissing a man you didn't know?"

Bewilderment, shock and indignation punctuated each comment. Samantha put her hand to her forehead. Her fingers automatically soothed the furrows. She couldn't explain who Jack Martin was or how she met him without digging herself in deeper.

"I know him, Mother. What I meant was that I don't know him well."

"Humph! You know him well enough to kiss him in public. That's enough for your father to insist you bring him home for a proper introduction. I'm not being critical, but I think you'd be much better off living at home while you're dating this young man. You know how aggressive these young men are today."

"Mother, I'm twenty-six, not fifteen."

"I'm perfectly aware of your age. I was at the hospital the day you were born." Her voice dropped. "Although I'll have to admit, there are times when I've wondered if there was some sort of a mix up."

"Did the premonition you called about have something to do with babies being switched?" Samantha teased in an effort to sidetrack her. "I don't think the hospital will take me back."

"I should hope not! Now that you've come to your senses and found a nice, respectable man to father my grandchildren—"

"From one kiss I'm going to get pregnant?" Samantha said, lacing her voice with shocked disbelief.

"Samantha, are you teasing me?"

"Yes, Mother."

Much as Sam loved her mother, during conversations of this nature, she wished her mother would sever her straight laces, remove her high-button shoes, let her hair down and join the women of the Twentieth century. Such wishes were pointless. Neither of them was going to change. To be brutally honest, Samantha admired her mother. Of the two of them, she knew her mother was the most content.

"Does this young man of yours have honorable intentions?"

"Marriage?"

"Certainly. You can't live like a flower child all your life."

"Mother," Samantha groaned, "the flower children bloomed years ago."

"Speaking of flowers, since you're dating this new fellow, you have broken up with that florist, haven't you?"

"Jacob? What's wrong with Jacob? He's single, attractive, financially secure."

"And he plays with flowers. Your dad says that only a sissy britches would raise flowers for a living."

Sam lifted her eyes to the ceiling, begging for deliverance. "Jacob doesn't raise flowers," Sam argued in defense of her friend. "He buys them, arranges them and sells them to men to bring home to their sweet wives."

"Your Dad brings me flowers and you bring me a pansy," Sam's mother quipped dryly, but knowing how staunchly loyal Sam was to her friends, she quickly said, "Back to the reason I called. Does your new young man like chicken and dumplings?"

"He prefers peanut butter and jelly."

"Oh dear! I do have a recipe for peanut butter cookies that calls for a dab of jelly on top. I suppose I could serve them for dessert."

"Mother, don't. I'll be there for dinner Sunday by myself."

"Darling, I hate being pushy, but don't you think we should meet him before the wedding?"

"I promise to bring the man I'm going to marry home in plenty of time for Dad to oil up the white shotgun."

"Samantha!"

"Just kidding, Mother."

"I should certainly hope so!"

"I'll see you Sunday."

"You will call if you decide to invite your fiancé, won't you?"

"Yes Mother. I love you."

As Samantha hung up the telephone, she suffered pangs of regret. Much as she loved her parents, she knew what a bewildering disappointment she'd been to her mother and father. Often she'd wondered if having brothers and sisters would have made a difference. The responsibility of having her parents' hopes pinned on her shoulders weighed heavily.

Melissa should have my problems, Sam thought, picking up a curved piece of wire and twirling it. Mother would understand her... I think.

Her lips twitched into a reluctant smile. Much as she moaned and groaned about her old-fashioned parents, Sam wouldn't have traded them for anyone. True, they didn't quite grasp where she came from. True, they were certain that unmarried women at her ripe old age were in the spinster category. And yet, they loved her, despite her faults. What more could a daughter want?

Much later in the day, Sam tossed her pliers on the worktable. She tilted her chair on its back legs and congratulated herself on a superproductive day. Not only was the toaster fixed, but also a pencil sharpener, a can opener, two electric clocks and a lamp.

She mentally calculated how much she'd made and felt twice as pleased. After fixing two or three more items she'd have more than enough for the utility bill. Looking forward to devoting the remainder of the afternoon to working on her special projects, she considered not answering the phone when it began to ring. The thought of the caller being a customer who wanted to pick up one of the items she'd repaired made her reconsider.

"Sam's Fixit Shop," she said cheerfully.

"Samantha, I'm glad you survived your dunking last night without any ill effects," Jack said with a smile in his voice. "This is Jack Martin."

"Jack Martin?" Samantha replied, pretending not to recognize the common name or the voice. Nothing deflated a man's ego like not recognizing his name.

"Yeah. The guy you were kissing on the newscast last night?"

The lilt in his voice sent shivers down her spine and goose bumps across her arms. Her mind conjured up his image with such clarity that she felt as though she could almost touch him.

"*That* Jack Martin! And I wasn't kissing you."

"So you've said." His voice lowered to an intimate pitch. "I've thought about you today."

His tone had the effect of a battering ram on her defenses. But not if her life depended on it would she make an admission similar to his. With the least bit of encouragement, she knew she'd be in over her head with Jack.

"You're supposed to say, 'Why Jack, sweetie pie, I thought about you, too.' I'm waiting."

"*Sweetie pie? Honey,* maybe, *sweetheart,* possibly, but *sweetie pie?*" Samantha asked.

"Any endearment would suffice," Jack countered.

"But what if I didn't think about you?" Liar, liar, Sam's pants on fire, she silently chastized herself, remembering how she'd held the trunks he'd worn in her hands and wondered if she'd see him again.

"You're being provocative, Samantha. Makes me want to make certain that the next time I call you'll vividly remember who I am."

"Okay, Jack. End-of-game strategy. Last night I tried to be subtle. Today, I'll use a sledgehammer. I'm not interested."

"Why?"

"Why?" Samantha repeated. He wasn't supposed to ask why.

"Am I physically repulsive to you?"

"Don't be ridiculous. You don't need me to flatter you by telling you that you're good-looking."

"Honey, with you I need all the flattery I can get. What is it about me that you do find repulsive?"

"Nothing. Honest. I'm simply not interested in any man."

"I'm glad to hear that, too. I'd hate to have some man brokenhearted over losing you."

Samantha felt like asking her mother's favorite question: "Are you kidding?" The thought of some man nursing a broken heart over her was ludicrous. She'd been the one who'd forsaken men rather than have chronic heart ailment.

"I'd like to take you out tonight."

"I'm working late."

"Tomorrow? Maybe go to Hermann Park for a picnic?"

She could almost feel the heat transmitted over the telephone wires by his slow, southern drawl. Biting her lip to make sure she didn't capitulate and accept his invitation, she shook her head. After a moment, she said, "No."

"How about dinner and a movie? You shouldn't work on Saturday night and you do have to eat."

"No." To her own ears her refusal was sounding weaker. Louder, firmer, she repeated, "No thank you. You saw the appliances I have to fix. I have to work."

"Sunday? Don't tell me you're working on Sunday, too."

"I go to my parents on Sunday for dinner."

Samantha thought she heard him mutter, "At least you get one decent meal a week," but couldn't be certain. She recalled the conversation with her mother and her demands regarding Jack. She could solve two problems with one solution, couldn't she?

"I don't suppose you'd want to go with me, would you?"

Jack paused. A man didn't remain a bachelor for thirty-two years by going to dinner at a woman's parents' house on the first date. His finger automatically slipped between his shirt collar and neck.

"Wouldn't you prefer Tony's?" he countered.

"I can't afford Tony's."

"I'm inviting you. I wouldn't expect you to pick up the bill."

"I always pay my share. No hassles at the front door that way."

She could tell by the strangled tone of his voice that he was squirming. He probably thinks my folks are as zany as I am, she mused, covering her mouth with her hand to keep from chuckling aloud. Boy, is he in for a surprise. By the time he munches down on his peanut-butter-and-jelly cookie, my parents will be humming the

"Wedding March" in two-part harmony. He'll break speed records getting me back to the shop.

Her heart skipped a beat at the thought of Jack being anxious to get rid of her. Was this what she wanted? The thought of never hearing from him should have pleased her. Instead, it left her wondering if she'd made a mistake by inviting him to her parents' house.

"In that case, I'll accept your invitation," he said. "What time?"

"We'd have to be there by four o'clock sharp. Is that inconvenient?"

"That's fine." Thinking out loud, he added. "An early evening with your parents, and then you and I can plan on—"

"Bringing me straight back to the shop." After her parents put him through the third degree, she might have to walk home. Knowing her folks, they'd probably invite the minister. "I think I ought to warn you about my parents."

"Like mother, like daughter? I'm certain nothing will surprise me."

His incorrect assumption irked Sam. It would serve him right to be met at the door by the minister. An impish smile turned her lips upward. "Oh, Jack," she crooned, "I'm certain my mother will just love you."

Jack laughed. "If she does, I hope it's hereditary," he teased. "What's your dad like?"

Samantha pictured her short, fiftyish, slightly balding father, who earned his living as a mechanic for a large General Motors dealership. Jack would expect him to be unconventional. A wicked gleam of mischief twinkled in her eyes as she answered, "I'm not allowed to tell anybody much about his work. He's a traveling man."

"Salesman? We should have a lot in common."

"Not exactly a salesman. He deals in weapons."
*White shotguns!* Her mind spun as she fabricated a
new, dashing image of her father.

"Works for the government?"

"Not exactly. He represents a group of men in Detroit."

Jack strung the clues together. Her father traveled for
a group of men in Detroit doing secretive work involv-
ing weapons.

Samantha heard Jack gasp and knew he'd arrived at
the conclusions she'd led him toward. He'd pegged her
father as a gun runner or a hit man. Either way, these
tidbits of misinformation would make Jack treat her
father with utmost respect.

"Don't mention my saying anything. Dad's touchy
about outsiders knowing. Usually Dad tells everyone
he's a mechanic."

"Thanks for inviting me, Samantha. For a moment
there, I thought I was going to have to barter an introduction to the technical advisor at O'Toole's for a date
with you."

"I don't barter my inventions." A hostile note entered her voice to indicate she didn't barter for dates,
either.

"Hey, wait a minute. I said, 'a date.' Don't get all
bristly. Guess I should have quit while I was ahead,
huh? Sunday at four?"

"Dress informally," she added, knowing her dad
worked in the garden on Sunday afternoons and would
not want to get spruced up for company. "Dad wears a
pin-striped suit when he's out of town. When he's home
he downplays his image. Jeans will be fine."

"I don't own jeans."

"You live in Texas and you don't own a pair of jeans? Not even the expensive kind that have some other man's name embroidered on them?"

"Nope. Not even a pair of designer jeans."

"Forget your sexy southern drawl then. You can't possibly be a Texan."

"Born and raised in Dallas."

"'Nuff said."

"You must pick up the *Houston City Magazine* and read that article on Houston versus Dallas. Houstonians drive Cadillacs and pick 'em up trucks, and people from Dallas drive Rolls-Royces and Mercedes. Sassy doesn't belong in either category."

Samantha laughed. She'd almost believed the article when she read it, but hearing Jack actually quote it made it seem preposterous. "You do wear a white collar."

"Which according to you is welded to the chain link fence around O'Toole's. By the way, when I met you, you weren't wearing *any* collar *or* jeans."

"Guess the report was wrong." After a moment, she whispered, "You don't think some northern snowbird wrote it to start trouble here in Texas, do you?"

"Honey, Houston could secede from Texas and I'd volunteer for the Houston brigade. You want me to wear jeans, that's what I'll wear." Pleased to hear her teasing and laughing, Jack decided to end their conversation on a lighthearted note. "See you Sunday, y'hear?"

"Sunday it is. By now."

Sam burst into giggles the moment she hung up the phone. The father she'd invented lived up to her serendipity reputation. Jack had been expecting her father to be strange. She'd made him different all right, but not the way Jack expected. With a little strategic planning before the dinner, she was certain to guarantee Jack a meal he'd never forget.

Serendipity Sam strikes again!

# Five

As Samantha rode with Jack in his late-model Ford, she clamped her lips together to keep from blurting out the truth. Although she'd reassured herself repeatedly since she'd talked to him that she was doing the right thing, after one look at Jack, she'd doubted her sanity. How could a man be utterly devastating in brand new jeans and a red plaid shirt? Why was she sitting like a dumb bunny waiting for the hatchet to fall?

She twisted her fingers around the strap of her purse to keep them from touching the knife-sharp crease in his denims.

This well-planned disaster was going to quietly blow up in her face unless she did something.

"Jack, about my parents, uh, my dad in particular." The little white lies she'd told knotted in her throat.

"I won't let him know you let the secret out of the bag," Jack reassured her, wondering exactly what he'd say to her father. "I appreciate your warning me in advance."

"I should have kept my mouth shut," Samantha gritted.

"No problem."

"Pretend I told you that he's a mechanic and nothing else."

"Stop worrying, Samantha." He withdrew one hand from the steering wheel and placed it over hers. "I can take care of myself. You're as nervous as a cat on a hot tin roof. Relax."

"I can't. Why don't you drop me off? I'll meet you at the shop later."

"Bartering? Instinct tells me you're trying to cancel your dinner invitation . . . again."

"Men's intuition? No such animal. Women are the intuitive variety of the human species." Sam didn't need intuition to predict the outcome of this dinner. Mentally she could hear the time bomb ticking.

"That's propaganda. Tell me what you do if a machine doesn't work?"

Half listening, Sam glanced from the window, wondering if she could jump from the car at the next stop sign and vanish without a trace.

"Fix it," she answered, rejecting the idea of being able to outrun Jack's car. Huffing and puffing, she'd arrive at the parking lot in front of the shop, and he'd be leaning against Sassy. Scratch that stroke of genius, she thought scornfully.

"Something isn't working properly, correct?"

"Uh-huh."

She'd given Jack the street name but not the house number. Maybe she could find a house that looked as though the owners were gone and have him stop there.

When no one answered the doorbell, she could pretend dismay at having fouled up the plans. Reasonable, Samantha thought.

"So in a very logical, precise manner, you take it apart and fix it. Inventors have logical minds. Do you realize nine-tenths of the decisions a businessman makes are based on intuition?" Jack chuckled. "We call it gut-level feeling, but it's the same as what you women refer to as woman's intuition."

Samantha found a major flaw in her plan. Her parents lived at the end of a circular court. Her mother would be watching for their arrival. The minute Sam got out of the car and headed toward the wrong house, her mother would be on the doorstep calling her name. Kaboom! The time bomb would explode.

"Samantha? Have you heard a word I've said?"

"Of course. Men have gut reactions and women have intuition," she quoted, searching for another escape route.

Jack wasn't convinced he had her attention. "That's why O'Toole Life Preservers didn't buy SAM trunks."

"I think I'm getting sick," Samantha said, resorting to the oldest lame excuse. She'd have Jack take her back to the shop. She'd get rid of him, call her mother, tell her to put a hold on the peanut butter cookies, hop in Sassy and avert the disaster.

"Are we near your house?"

*Too near!* "No. Pull over."

"What's wrong?" Jack followed her order, parking the car on the side of the steeet.

"I'm getting a migraine. You'd better take me back to the shop."

"Migraines are caused by stress."

"Believe me, I'm under stress."

Jack looped his arm around her shoulders and drew her against his chest. She fits perfectly, he thought, loving her light spring fragrance and the soft supple feeling of her skin beneath his fingers.

"Is this the first time you've invited a man to your parents' house for dinner?"

"No, but this is different."

Samantha's hand found its way to the back of his neck. Confusion reigns supreme, she thought as she caressed the short dark hair. Here she was embracing the man she'd set up to meet her dad—the hit man!

"Why don't we go to your parents'. You take a couple of aspirin and lie down, and I'll chat with them until you're feeling better."

"No!" Samantha squeaked against the wall of his chest. Her nose nuzzled against the dark hairs in the open vee of his shirt. "I mean..." She couldn't think with one of his arms wrapped around her and the other stroking her back soothingly. "My dad doesn't travel as much as I told you. He's home most of the time."

Jack's stomach quivered as her forearm grazed against it when she wrapped her arm around his waist. She was doing crazy things to his libido.

"And Dad doesn't use weapons, exactly, unless you consider a car a lethal weapon. The men he works for out of Detroit? General Motors."

There! She'd confessed. Her breath feathered against the side of his neck. She noticed his quick intake of air. His pulse beat rapidly at the base of his throat.

"Your dad is a car salesman?"

"A mechanic. I exaggerated."

"Why?"

Jack raised her face. Her lips were parted. The tip of her tongue nervously wet them.

"Good question," she whispered, unable to think of anything other than how his lips would taste.

"Who cares why," he sighed, lowering his head.

*I care,* Samantha acknowledged silently. She didn't want to care about Jack Martin. She wanted the simple life. Becoming involved with Jack would end in heartache. Disillusionment. Why was she so thoroughly enjoying his kiss when she should be pushing him back across the width of the car?

For a moment, Jack felt her arms stiffen, as though she were preparing to push herself away. Then her arms wound tightly around him. Through the thin fabric of his cotton shirt he could feel the tips of her breasts harden. Her lips opened to him.

Jack's orderly mind short-circuited. He forgot about where they were, who her father was, when they were expected for dinner. His entire mind was focused on how good she felt and tasted.

He leaned back against the car door, sliding his leg on the seat as he cradled her more fully against himself. His hands, at first timidly, then with increasing boldness, slid from her hips. Deep in his throat he silently groaned as his fingers massaged her supple body.

His tongue delved deeper. The velvet rasp of hers combined with her gentle sipping of encouragement made the blood pound in his ears.

A wolf whistle from a passing motorist went barely noticed for several seconds. Finally the shrill sound registered. He straightened the curve of his back as he remembered they were on a busy street in broad daylight. Much as he hated to stop, he lovingly stroked her bottom lip with the tip of his tongue to reseal the treasure he'd discovered.

"Samantha?" His voice sounded shaky to his own ears. "I'm mussing you."

"Mussing?" she murmured dreamily, still caught in the enchantment of his very thorough kiss.

Seeing her lips, slightly swollen, nearly undid Jack for a second time. One of us has to come to our senses, he thought. He wound an errant lock of her blond hair around his finger. Brushing his lips across her golden-tipped lashes, he whispered, "Your dad will shoot me if I bring you to his house all mussed."

At the mention of her father, Samantha's eyes fluttered open. Her mouth worked, but speech was impossible. All she could see was the tiny embers of passion in his eyes being slowly brought under control.

"How's your migraine?" His thumb and forefinger rubbed the silky curl beside her temple.

Samantha gave him a shaky smile. "I think your 'mussing' should be marketed as a miracle drug."

"There's a mirror on the back side of the sun visor," he said, but his fingers continued to hold her captive. He realized he should let go of her. They were already late. He longed to turn off the sunlight, whisk her away to a hidden corner of the world and make love to her. "Samantha..."

Sam heard the tone of regret as he voiced her name. How could he regret kissing me? she wondered, instantly defensive. Had her chaste life-style made her kissing inept? She freed her hair from his fingers with a toss of her head.

"We'd better get going to my parents."

Her icy reply was more effective than a slap. Awkwardly he resumed his position behind the wheel. "I'm not going to apologize," he stated through clenched teeth.

Samantha flipped down the visor. Pretending to concentrate on restoring order to her disheveled hair, she hid the wounded look in her eyes. "You have nothing to apologize for."

"One of us is stark raving crazy," Jack muttered under his breath.

Her temper flared to protect her heart. "It's me. I'm a nut! I've always marched to the beat of my own drum. That's exactly what I've been telling you since you insisted on making me pay you for jumping into the pool!"

"No," he argued quietly. "It's me. You've affected my brain!"

"Stick around," she promised. "Right after dinner the whole family sings looney tunes!"

Jack pulled away from the curb without signaling or looking in the rearview mirror. A horn blared. Tires shrieked. Samantha was pitched forward, but Jack's arm shot out protectively, bracing her against the seat.

"I'm sorry. I didn't look where I was going."

She realized his quick reflexes had saved her from a nasty bump. But the intimacy of having his arm locked across her breasts after he'd regretted kissing her sent an electrical charge straight to her toes. All ten of them curled under.

Jack removed his arm. Seeing how pale she was, he asked, "Are you okay?"

"I'm going to be fine," she predicted, uncurling her toes. Before the evening was over, she was going to show Jack Martin she could muss up his mind with her kisses. She might have put her feminine wiles on hold for several years, but she had faith in the quality of her equipment. She was a woman, by the grace of God, and he'd know it before midnight! O'Toole Life Preservers, Inc.

had rejected her SAM trunks, but O'Toole's plant manager wasn't going to be allowed to reject Samantha Ann Mason.

"Which house?" Jack asked, turning left onto Trowbridge Court.

"The one with the lady standing on the porch waving her handkerchief." Samantha would have been chagrined by her mother's open display of anticipation under other circumstances. Even now, she had the urge to sink farther back into the seat. Chin thrust forward, Samantha reached over Jack's arm and blew the horn to herald their arrival and called out the window, "Hi, Mom! I've brought him home to meet you."

Before Jack had time to turn off the motor, she bounded from the car and went up the steps.

Maxine Mason clapped her hands together gleefully. She knew by the way her daughter had stressed *him* that this man was her daughter's choice of matrimonial bliss. She hugged Samantha.

"Handsome devil, isn't he?" Samantha said loudly enough for Jack to hear. "Where's Dad?"

"Washing his hands for dinner. Come and introduce me."

Jack closed his door, wondering what the heck was going on. Samantha was driving him crazy with her I-hate-you, I-love-you signals. He could have sworn she'd wanted to scratch his eyes out just minutes ago. Now she was referring to him as handsome.

"Jack, this is my mother, Maxine."

Samantha grinned as she watched her mother avoid Jack's outstretched hand and step up to hug him like a long lost son. Her smile broadened when Jack seemingly didn't know what to do with his hands. She heard her father coming down the steps.

"Jack, this is my father, Clifford."

Maxine stepped back, her face flushed with excitement. "This is *him*!"

"I'm glad to meet you, Son." Clifford grabbed Jack's hand in both of his and enthusiastically pumped it up and down. "Come in. We've been waiting for you."

Samantha smothered a giggle. Her mother and father were two people she could count on to behave in a predictable manner. With the right cues coming from his daughter, Clifford would bring the shotgun into the living room to oil it in front of Jack. No beating around the bush where her father was concerned.

The first day they'd met she'd said, "no, no, no," to Jack. That hadn't worked. He'd persisted until she'd weakened and invited him to her parents' for dinner. Can't take no for an answer, she mused, watching how Jack's back stiffened as her father gave him a vigorous clap on the shoulder. How about a fervent "yes, yes, yes?"

"Nice to meet you both," Jack said. Had his first suspicions about why Samantha had invited him to her parents' house for dinner been correct? Was she clever enough to challenge him, thwart him, then lead him to the altar before he knew what was happening?

"I fixed a special dinner for you, Jack," Maxine chattered, leading the way into the house. "Samantha told me you love peanut butter and jelly. Clifford, why don't you take Jack into the living room. Sam, could you help me in the kitchen for a minute?"

Clifford pounded Jack on the back. "Well, Son, what do you do for a living?"

Using his bachelor's dictionary, Jack translated the inquiry as, "Can you support my daughter?" He shot Samantha a piercing look.

Samantha purposely rounded her cornflower blue eyes into an expression of perfect innocence. She had to control the urge to overplay her part by grabbing Jack's hand and planting a wet kiss on the palm.

"Sam, he's precious!" Maxine squealed once they were behind the kitchen door. "I couldn't have picked a better man for you myself. So...rugged looking."

It was one thing to bamboozle Jack, but another to raise false hopes in her mother. "Mom, don't count on anything. Jack and I barely know one another."

"Don't kid me. I saw how you looked at him. Remember the time you worked on that contraption to make a bike sound like a motorcycle? Well, my dear, when it finally roared to life there was a certain gleam in your eye. I saw that same gleam a minute ago."

Sam opened the oven and sniffed. From the odor, she expected to find a Jolly-Green-Giant-size peanut. How could a ham look like a ham and smell like a peanut?

"Ham with a special sauce," Maxine said.

"A special sauce made with peanut butter?" Sam asked, her stomach churning at the thought of spreading peanut butter on a ham sandwich. Yuck!

"You won't believe how many recipe books I searched through before I found that recipe."

"I believe you," Samantha groaned. She moved to the stove. "Green beans?"

"Do you think a few dry-roasted peanuts would liven up the taste?"

"No. I think Jack takes his beans straight. What can I do to help?"

"Oh, nothing, dear. I just wanted to give your dad a chance to have a man-to-man with Jack."

"More like a father-to-prospective-son-in-law talk? Isn't that what you mean?"

"Samantha Ann Mason! We've waited forever to see you come to your senses and settle down with a nice young man. Don't deprive us of a single glorious moment!" Maxine tossed Samantha a pot holder. "You could put the ham on the platter. Be sure you save the sauce. Once the ham is sliced, Jack will probably want to use it as gravy."

After Samantha managed to get the ham on the platter, she took it into the dining room. Hard as she tried, she couldn't distinguish what her father was saying to Jack in the living room. A couple of times, she heard them chuckle. Tiptoeing to the doorway that separated the two rooms, she carefully listened.

"Sam!" her mother whispered in a familiar tone of chastisement. "Eavesdroppers never hear good things about themselves!"

"Who? Me? Eavesdrop? It's so quiet in there. What are they doing?'

Maxine shrugged. "Probably browsing through the family picture albums."

"You're kidding! You didn't bring out those old pictures!"

"Of course I did. You told me you didn't know each other well. By the time he gets to the snapshot—"

"Mother!" Horrified, Sam raced into the living room.

Both men started to rise.

"Sam, I'm glad you came in here. Who's wedding were you the bridesmaid in when you wore the frilly pink dress?"

"Amanda Fielding's." Her none too subtle father had chosen the bridesmaid album out of a choice of twenty or thirty other albums. "Dinner is served."

"Thanks, Clifford, for sharing Samantha's pictures with me. I think my favorite album was the one with the baby shots." As Jack passed through the door he lightly pinched Samantha's rosy red cheeks. "Some birthday suit," he said, chuckling.

Samantha could have cheerfully smacked both of them. There was no doubt in her mind what Jack was referring to—the series of pictures taken on her second birthday. Her father had set the cake on the high chair and she'd helped herself. She could almost see the chocolate icing smeared in her hair and on the ribbon flattened on her nearly bald head. But, that wasn't the worst picture. Her mother had stripped her of her clothing and taken her outside to wash her down with the hose! At the time, she must have relished running through the back yard naked as the day she was born.

But now?

Samantha blushed from her toes to her scalp. Knowing her father, she knew he'd made the same comments to Jack that he always made whenever those pictures were shown: "Look at those cute dimples on her fanny." And her mother would add, "And those cute chubby legs."

"Don't be embarrassed, Sam," her father said, grinning from ear to ear. "Jack enjoyed them. Didn't you, Son?"

Jack held a chair for Samantha. "Most revealing," he teased.

Sam wanted to slide down the chair and under the table, and pull the table cloth with her.

"How were the snacks?" Maxine inquired over her shoulder as Jack seated her.

"Superb." He cast Samantha a meaningful smile. "Little squares of toast lightly spread with chunky peanut butter and grape jelly. How sweet of you to tell your mother."

Sam had to give Jack credit. He ate two helpings of everything and managed to keep his tongue from sticking to the top of his mouth long enough to carry on an intelligent conversation. He charmed her mother by praising the dinner and flattered her father by talking about how reliable Chevys are.

With each sticky mouthful of ham, Sam was certain beyond the wildest doubt that poetic justice had to be flavored with peanut butter sauce.

She was also certain that her grandiose plan of reducing Jack to mush with one soul-blasting kiss wouldn't work either. The sauce would probably permanently bond them together!

Watching her father beam and her mother preen, Sam realized how happy she'd made them by inviting Jack to dinner. This was what they'd expected when they'd dressed her in Polly Flanders dresses years ago. They weren't asking for anything other than a standard, normal daughter who would bring home a charming husband and, in time, a few equally charming grandchildren.

Why couldn't she live up to their expectations?

Sam couldn't honestly answer the question, though she'd asked it a million times. "I am what I am" seemed to be an unbearably selfish code of conduct. Heaping condemnation upon condemnation, she added Jack's name to her growing list of failures.

He'd told her she was driving him crazy. To Sam, that was natural. She'd driven all her boyfriends crazy. But not intentionally, she mused, not the way she had treated Jack. From the moment they'd met, she'd doused him with cold water both literally and figuratively.

She stared at Jack. Persistent, she surmised. Stubborn as a Missouri mule. Could he persevere through her flashes of creative genius? How would he react to forgetfulness, broken dates, days when she buried herself in the back room of her shop?

Jack smiled at something her father said. The smile lingered as he met her stare.

*I could fall in love with you,* Samantha thought. Would that bold streak of persistence protect us from hurting each other?

As though he read her mind, he said, "Yes."

"Fried ice cream for you, dear?" Maxine asked.

"The gooey kind with hard ice cream on the inside and a caramel peanut sauce poured on top," Clifford added.

"With whipped cream?" Samantha asked.

Jack nudged his foot between hers. "And lots and lots of nuts."

# Six
---

"Do your parents always act as though your dinner guest is the bridegroom at the rehearsal dinner?" Jack asked once he'd backed from the driveway and headed toward Sam's shop.

Samantha grinned. "Not what you expected?"

"Hardly."

"What did you expect?"

Jack thoughtfully rubbed his chin, pondering a tactful reply. "Older versions of you."

"I'm a throwback. Dad's grandmother kept her crazy inventions in the attic." Chuckling, Samantha amended, "Or do I have that backwards? Dad's grandmother was crazy and confined to the attic with her inventions? She's the least spoken about member of his family."

"Are any of her inventions patented?"

"Are you serious? At the turn of the century, women didn't have the right to vote, much less acquire a patent." Samantha shook her head. "Any skeletons in the Martin closet?"

"I come from a long line of organizers. Even back then when birth control was only whispered about, the Martins managed to deliver their babies in September."

"Virgo?"

"Yep. Astrology may be bunk, but I'd give five-to-one odds that you're a Gemini."

"May twelfth."

Jack smiled. "A Gemini. You don't happen to have a twin lurking around somewhere, do you?"

"I've often wished that I did. Someone *normal* for my parents to dote on."

"You aren't abnormal. A little wacky around the edges, maybe, but definitely within the boundaries of normal."

"Sometimes I feel like two people inside one body," she admitted. "I've tried being what my parents expected, but..."

"You don't fit into the mold?"

"Exactly. Don't discount their treating you as a prospective son-in-law. They haven't given up hope. Though Lord knows I've given them plenty of reason."

Sam's hands twisted in her lap. What was she doing explaining herself to Jack? she wondered. She'd decided long ago to quit apologizing for who and what she was. She'd been strong enough to reject Jack's advances, but she hadn't been able to prevent herself from thinking about what she'd been missing. There isn't room in my life for that type of weakness, she silently chastised herself. Becoming aware that her fingernails had burrowed into her palms, she unclenched her hands.

"Parents expect the best for their offspring. Fortunately I have an older brother who fits my parents' idea of a captain of industry. Grant started a shoestring operation as an electrical supplier, and now he runs one of the biggest supply houses in Dallas."

"Your job isn't anything to sneeze at. What would your parents think if you lived in the back of a shop and bartered your way through life?"

"They know how determined I am. Within five years, they'd expect me to successfully market one of those million-dollar ideas."

"Could you?" Sam struggled to keep the note of hopefulness out of her voice.

"Perhaps. I'd go about it completely different than you have."

Jack pulled into the strip shopping center parking lot and parked the car. Turning toward Samantha, he discovered wary anticipation written on her face.

"How?"

"Well, let's take the letters you sent to various life jacket manufacturers."

"You take them," Samantha quipped. "I have another stack somewhere around the shop."

Reaching across the seat, Jack snagged a handful of her unruly blond hair and lightly massaged his fingers into it until he touched the warmth of her scalp. She edged closer. The fragrance of her floral shampoo teased his senses.

"Get serious, Sam."

"I am serious," Samantha replied, attempting to wiggle closer. "Rejection slips are a dime a dozen at Sam's Fixit Shop."

"You're sending your letters to the wrong places."

The silky, fine texture of her hair slid through his fingers. Again, his fingers delved into the elusive strands. This time, several short curly locks clung to his fingers.

"Logically, who would be the most interested in buying SAM trunks. The trunks are untried, untested and unproven. Do you think a company would abandon a product that was tried and tested and proven to put cash in the till to market SAM trunks?"

"But my invention is better! They'll make millions!"

"Perhaps. But, while they're promoting SAM trunks, they're systematically destroying the sale of standard vests."

"I hadn't thought of it in that perspective." Jack's hand was gently stroking the back of her head, making rational thought difficult. The sensuous twin inside Sam craved closer contact. Sam the inventor could thrive on a cerebral diet of flashes of genius, but Samantha the woman yearned for physical contact.

"Have you seen those little inflatable things kids put on their arms when they're learning how to swim?"

"Hmmm. Water wings," she answered.

"Toy manufacturers market them, not a company like O'Toole's."

Jack felt himself sinking into the blueness of Samantha's eyes. What in the world was he doing discussing marketing strategies when all he wanted to do was make love to her? He closed his eyes to quiet the sound of his heartbeat, which was thudding loudly in his ears.

"SAM trunks aren't a toy."

"They won't qualify as a life preserver. Water Safety Council approval depends on head support. You have to keep the victim from drowning."

"Couldn't a company like O'Toole's market them as a recreational line? For nonswimmers who want to fool around in water over their head?"

Samantha, like a nonswimmer in sixty-foot-deep water, sucked a draft of air into her lungs, hoping to clear her head of the dizzy sensation his fingers were causing. His magical touch was destroying her anxiety to sell her million-dollar idea.

Womanly ideas formed in her mind and slowly percolated through her bloodstream to her heart.

At her parents' house she'd realized how easily she could fall in love with Jack. Now, Samantha became aware of how much she wanted him.

Her eyes closed and her hands framed his face as she tactilely memorized the feel of his strong, square jaw covered with fine sandpaper whiskers. Her fingers moved upward, tracing the width of his brow, the straightness of his nose, the height of his prominent cheekbones. Her fingers quivered as they lingered on the well-defined line of his upper lip. One thumb traced the puckered bow below. He expelled a deep breath, warming her exploring fingers.

"Samantha? Are you thinking about how I would market SAM trunks?" The hoarse quality of his voice revealed the effect her curious fingers had on him.

"Uh-uh. I'm thinking about how good it feels to touch you, wondering if you'd regret kissing me this time."

Jack's hands slipped to Samantha's shoulders. Hauling her against his chest, he demanded, "Who regretted that kiss? Certainly not me!"

"I heard it in your voice."

"I may have regretted having a dinner engagement that prevented me from pursuing where the kiss was leading to, but I swear I never regretted kissing you."

Samantha's eyes flicked open. The honesty that she'd come to recognize shone in his eyes. "I must have misunderstood."

Giving her shoulders a sharp shake, Jack said, "Keep your eyes open."

"Why?"

"Because I want you to take a good look at Jack Martin. You only believe what you see, not what you feel. What do you see?"

"You," she responded simply, refusing to verbalize the emotions she could read in the expression on his face.

"Do you see a man who's casually interested in dating you?"

"I don't know."

Jack's fingers tightened around her arm. "Look again."

For long moments they silently communicated with their eyes locked.

At first, Samantha tried to avoid comprehending the meaning. The dark centers of his eyes widened, drawing her into their depths. There was no hiding from the leashed passion she saw. But there was something else, something beyond her comprehension, something she'd never seen before.

Jack watched her expression change from understanding to bewilderment. "Sam, you've warned me about yourself, now let me warn you. Virgos are fastid-ious. They don't enter into casual, one-night stands. My gut reaction tells me we need to talk more than we needed to make love, but . . .''

He no longer could resist. Primitive instinct de-manded he erase the bewildered confusion he knew she was feeling. His head descended. His lips claimed hers more roughly than he'd intended.

Momentarily she pushed against his chest, as though to reject him. Jack knew the twins, Sam and Saman-tha, were at war. Sam resented his physical domina-tion, but Samantha relished it. Within a breath, Samantha won. Her elbows unlocked. Her arms cir-cled his shoulders, straining to bring him closer within the confines of the car.

Sam asserted herself by probing between Jack's lips with the tip of her tongue. His taste flooded her senses. A nutty flavor blended with the sweetness of honey and passion brought her a moment of sweet, mindless ex-hilaration. Just as she had blindly memorized his facial features, she now imprinted his taste on her mind. Her head tilted backward as he sheathed her tongue, sip-ping as she had sipped earlier, drawing her deeper into himself. With a sigh that came from intimate discov-ery, she enticed him to reciprocate, to explore her sweetness.

Samantha Ann Mason was a blend of both Sam and Samantha. She dominated, she submitted. Jack al-lowed her the freedom to do both.

She was his equal.

"Take me inside," Jack implored, stringing a line of heated kisses along the column of her neck.

"The shop?"

"The shop. You. Lord woman, I want you so badly I ache."

"The shop's a mess."

Jack rocked his forehead against hers. "I promise. I won't notice." His hand climbed from her waist to the underside of her breast. "Kisses aren't enough for either of us. Admit it."

Glancing at the yellow neon light that blinked, Sam's Fixit Shop, she shuddered. The only thing she could admit were her flaws. By the time they cleared the sofa bed, opened it and changed the sheets, Jack's ardor would have cooled to disdain.

A sharp pain stabbed her chest. An inkling that Jack's persistence would rapidly wane and she'd have to face another rejection tangled her thoughts.

Jack felt her physically and mentally withdraw. "No! What's going on in that pretty head of yours. Tell me."

"You're fastidious. I'm a slob. It will take half an hour to straighten the bed enough to..." Being crushed against Jack's chest ended her explanation.

"Dammit, Sam. You incinerate me with your passion, then reduce me to a heap of ashes by wanting to please me by being a neatnik. I want you as you are, Samantha. You don't have to change for me."

Hesitating, feeling vulnerable and yet at the same time bold, she asked, "Could we go to your place?"

Jack held her tightly. During the short drive to his condominium would she think up a dozen reasons for them not to be together? As sure as the summer sun was hot, he knew himself well enough to know his control would explode if she hesitated at the last moment.

He wanted her.

"Sweetheart, I'm beyond caring whether we make love in the back seat, in a messy shop, at my place or on the moon. I just don't think I could survive the night without loving you.''

Samantha related to that feeling. "Are you worried about me changing my mind at the last minute?" His cheek moved up and down against hers. She smiled. "I won't change my mind. Inventors are known for their stick-to-itiveness.''

Playfully nibbling her ear, Jack whispered, "As long as it's me you're sticking to, I won't object.''

"I always finish what I start. Sometimes—'' she shrugged backward as his hold loosened "—I don't anticipate the results, but I always complete the project.''

Jack smiled. "Serendipity?''

"Your meaning, not mine. But maybe the definition will change.''

As Jack tenderly kissed her, Sam fervently wished the fiery flames of their desire would chemically alter the genes her great-grandmother had passed on to her. She didn't want to be locked up in the attic or, more precisely, in her Fixit Shop.

She cuddled against Jack during the long minutes it took to get to his place. In the dark silence she convinced herself that this time she wouldn't fail. Jack knew her flaws. She hadn't misrepresented herself. He'd accept the good with the bad. Jack wouldn't become another water blanket.

"Do you have a water bed?''

"Why?'' Jack drove with his left hand and held Samantha with his right.

"I invented a water blanket using the same principles as an electric blanket.''

"And tried to sell it to an electric blanket manufacturer, right?''

# ...be tempted!

**See inside for special
4 FREE BOOKS offer**

*Silhouette Desire*®

# A FREE
## Folding Umbrella
### *and* Mystery Gift
#### *await you, too!*

← Clip and mail this postpaid card today! ↙

**Mail this card today for**

**4 FREE BOOKS**
(a $9.00 value)
**this Folding Umbrella and
a Mystery Gift *ALL FREE!***

*Clip and mail this postpaid card today!*

## Silhouette Desire ®

**Silhouette Books, 120 Brighton Rd., P.O. Box 5084, Clifton, NJ 07015-9956**

☐ **YES!** Please send me my four Silhouette Desire novels along with my FREE Folding Umbrella and Mystery Gift, as explained in this insert. I understand that I am under no obligation to purchase any books.

NAME _____ (please print)

ADDRESS _____

CITY _____ STATE _____ ZIP _____

Terms and prices subject to change.
Your enrollment is subject to acceptance by Silhouette Books.

Silhouette Desire is a registered trademark.

CAD086

"Right." Samantha squeezed his thigh. "You didn't answer my question. Do you have a water bed?"

"As a matter of fact, I do. So help me, Sam, if you tell me you get seasick, we won't make it through the living room."

"Serve you right if I did. I caught that subtle dig about marketing my water blanket. Do you know what one manufacturer had the nerve to call my idea?"

"Technical advisors aren't known for tactfulness in their rejection letters."

"Some idiot nicknamed it a wet blanket." Samantha heard a strangled sound and felt his sides shake. "Are you laughing?"

"I'm trying not to laugh," Jack admitted when Sam's light squeeze threatened to change into a pinch. He squawked before he was injured, "Ouch."

"My exact sentiments."

"You have to give the guy some credit for imagination. He could have sent you a standard rejection letter."

"And while I'm benevolently giving him credit, where should I forward my next letter?"

Jack grinned. "I'd have to think about that. Right now, my mind is on other ways to keep people warm in bed."

Samantha whispered something deliciously naughty but decidedly unfeasible in his ear.

"Sweetheart, your inventiveness isn't confined to the back room of the shop, is it?"

"Let's hope not," she replied, her eyes twinkling mischievously. "Don't be surprised if I come up with a novel idea by morning."

"Let's not wish the night away by being in a rush for sunrise."

Jack turned off NASA 1 highway into a private parking lot. As he parked the car in his assigned place, he watched Samantha's face. Although the condominium project wasn't as ritzy as others located on Clear Lake, his home was a far cry from living in the back of the Fixit Shop.

"Impressive," Sam muttered, thinking the down payment on his condo would have financed six months to a year's experimentation on her Turn Off the Light project. She couldn't help thinking in dollars and cents. She knew even the most successful inventors scrimped to finance their projects.

"I'm glad you like it. The balcony overlooks Clear Lake. Come on."

Jack took Samantha's hand as she scooted under the steering column. When she stood beside him, he swept one arm under her knees and lifted her into his arms.

Sam squirmed, unaccustomed to being swept off her feet.

"Don't," Jack said, grinning. "I'm not a highly imaginative man, but carrying you into my home greatly appeals to me."

"Caveman tactics?"

Jack stopped long enough to silence her jibe with a hearty kiss. "Whatever."

"Man's way of showing the little woman she can't get anywhere on her own two feet?" Samantha prodded, offering her lips for another kiss.

Laughing, Jack shook his head. "Your logic is going to get you flat on your back before we reach the bedroom," he quipped, realizing she was teasing him with more than her words.

"Hmmm. Flat on my back? Leave it to a successful businessman to want to be on top of everything."

Even in the dim light coming from the quarter moon, Jack could see the impish light in her eyes. With one swift motion, he lightly tossed her over his shoulder into a fireman's carry.

"Jack!"

"This, my dear, is how a domineering man carts his woman into his cave. Like it?"

"Jack, you put me down!" Samantha covered her giggles with her hand. "What will your neighbors think!"

"Want me to ring doorbells as I go down the hall?"

"Don't you dare!"

"I hate to disappoint you, but each condo has a private entrance." Jack unlocked his door, then slowly eased her from his shoulder. He held her against his chest, with her feet inches from the floor. His smile turned serious when he saw how flushed her face was. "You okay?"

Samantha grinned as she mimed hitting him squarely in the jaw. "That's what a man would do to you if you carted him upside down."

"But sweetheart, you're all woman." His hands cupped her derriere as he lowered her until her toes touched the carpet.

"All woman," Sam repeated, suddenly aware of the contrast between the softness of her body and the hardness of his. "And glad of it," she whispered, stepping backward, leading, rather than following, him into his condo.

As though preprogrammed, Samantha led him through the living room, down the hallway, into the master suite. The bedside lamp lit her way.

Jack contented himself with allowing her to, as she put it, come in under her own power. Only in jest would he play the role of dominant lover. Her unique blend of femininity and independence intrigued him. He'd do nothing to destroy it.

For no logical reason, Samantha shivered with apprehension. From the beginning, she'd given the impression of being an experienced woman. She wasn't. And Jack was about to discover exactly how limited her experience was.

Worldly women were prepared for any eventuality. Much as she wanted Jack, she was a scientist of sorts and knew what the end product of a careless night of lovemaking could be.

"I'll protect you." He'd watched her nervously glance from the bed to her stomach. "I'll always protect you as best I can."

If Samantha hadn't already fallen in love with him, she would have then. Jack seldom did anything without forethought. Protecting his woman was no exception. She'd be safe with him.

Secure in that knowledge, she reached behind her back, caught the flap of the zipper between her fingers and slowly pulled it down. She heard his appreciative intake of breath as the bodice yielded to the pull of gravity. The dress fell into a heap at her feet. She stooped, picked it up, and lightly tossed it on a nearby chair.

She watched Jack's dark eyes grow even more intense. Clad only in her lacy bra, half-slip and bikini pants, she narrowed the gap between them. "I'll undress you."

Jack shook his head as though in a trance. He'd known she'd be beautiful. He'd seen her in skimpier clothing back at Astro Hall. Still, he wasn't prepared for the exquisite torture of having her modestly remove her clothing with a feline grace all her own. She hadn't changed her mind, and yet, he felt fragile. Explosive. His desire switched from wanting to please himself to desperately wanting to give pleasure.

For the first time in his life that he could remember, he allowed a woman to take the initiative, to undress him. Her fingers loosened his tie and stripped it from his neck. He didn't notice where she tossed it or where it landed. Buttons. He counted them, straining impatiently for her light touch on his chest. She shed his jacket and shirt with one deft movement.

Sam hesitated.

He wanted her to continue badly enough to beg. "Please, don't stop."

Samantha raised her hands to his chest. The dark, crisp hairs on his chest reminded her of those at the back of his neck. Ever so slowly her hands descended until they rested on his belt. She felt his lean stomach quiver beneath her fingers. Then he sucked it in to accommodate her unbuckling his belt.

A surge of heady power made her hand tremble. As though struck by lightning, she suddenly realized that Jack had taken her joking seriously. She'd teased him regarding his male image. By remaining immobile, he was proving she controlled the situation. He wouldn't pounce on her, demanding instant male gratification. He would make love *with* her, not *to* her. The joy of intimacy would be mutual. Equal.

Dark desire in his eyes hungrily met the sky blue intensity of Samantha's eyes. His pulse soared as her fingers mastered the task of removing his belt, of unhooking the waistband of his slacks. Tooth by tooth she lowered the zipper.

Only when she'd accomplished the task did he realize he'd held his breath, uncertain he'd survive her leisurely pace. He swallowed hard. His knees threatened to collapse as he stumbled toward Samantha.

"I'm as nervous as a kid," he mumbled, endearing himself to her.

Samantha confessed her insecurity. "I'm inexperienced, but I want to please you."

"Samantha, you please me." He held her hand over his heart. "Feel. It's pounding. My whole insides are pulsating."

Their mouths came together as her arms twined around his shoulders and she fitted herself into the cradle of his pelvis. Heat and fire consumed them until there wasn't time for rational thought. Both reacted to primitive drives.

His hands raced over her shoulders, waist and buttocks in a frenzy of tactility. Her heated flesh made his hands sure as they deftly unhooked her bra, freeing her breasts from confinement. His mouth freed hers as he placed hot, moist kisses downward, allowing his thumbs the liberty of removing her remaining underthings.

"Jack..." She whispered permission, encouragement, by speaking his name.

Samantha's back arched as his lips and tongue circled the tips of her breasts. Although she dug her fingers into his shoulders in response to the delicious tingling sensation, she felt herself falling until she gently landed in the center of his water bed.

She felt euphoric as she discovered each variance of texture, flavor and color detailing his taut frame. As he made similar explorations, she felt her need build.

Slowly he carried her hand downward. "Touch me?"

Her fingers sensuously circled his navel. Jack moaned his sense of urgency as she intimately brushed against him. She could have shyly denied him what he sought. He would have let her. And yet, the budding love growing in her heart was justification for investigating all of him.

"Oh, Samantha...sweetheart..." Jack gasped as his entire body shuddered under her butterfly soft touch. His hand touched her, his palm stroking the slight mound as his fingers entered the warmth below.

Samantha's response was impetuous, uninhibited.

"Yessss," Jack hissed, his eyes squeezing shut at her candid response. Her shouting his name inflamed him, but his sense of responsibility prevailed. He protected her from pregnancy.

Then his possession was swift. His hips rolled, thrusting madly.

In wild abandon, Samantha matched his ferocity. A trail of prickles climbed from her ankles, up her calves, over the front of her thighs, ending in a convulsive explosion deep inside her.

Jack held her hips as he too reached his peak. He buried his face against the damp curls nestled on her fevered neck.

Unrestrained joy bubbled from within Samantha as laughter expressed her fulfillment.

He understood. Just as she'd artlessly shouted his name, she voiced her happiness with laughter. His chuckles matched hers.

For Sam there would be no self-recrimination. No guilt trip. No asking herself in the early hours of the morning as the sun seemed to burst from beneath the lake, 'What have I done?' She accepted ecstasy. To her, it was a part of being alive, of being who she was.

"Oh, my gosh. Was that me screaming?" Samantha asked as Jack rolled to his side but remained a part of her.

"Ummm-hmmm. Unexpected but delightful."

Samantha didn't know how to explain the feeling of bliss surrounding her. She'd never experienced it before but she was compelled to speak, just as after completing a difficult experiment she was compelled to jot down notes.

"I feel giddy. Like I've created something fantastic."

Jack grinned. "Maybe in the grand scheme of things that's why mating leads to little bundles of joy," he teased.

"Sounds logical to me." Her hand followed the hollow at his waist to his hip.

"What about babies?"

Her fingers flexed as they touched the firm muscle of his upper thigh. He drew his knee over her hip, locking them together.

"Soft. Cuddly." Her brows rose. "You aren't thinking of . . . ?"

"You are an inventor. What could you create that would—" His laughter interrupted his speech as she tickled the back of his knee.

"I think, my dear Jonathan 'Jack' Martin, that the patent office would refuse to grant a patent on such an invention. That's not exactly a new idea!"

"Isn't it?"

He brushed tendrils of blond hair from her forehead as Samantha pondered his question. Yes, she admitted silently, to her it was a completely innovative idea, one she hadn't considered.

"I'm not certain a baby would meet the criteria an inventor requires," she responded loftily.

"Be specific."

"Well, first of all, there has to be a flash of genius. Now I admit that flashes of brilliant color burst on my eyelids when we made love, but..."

Her thought trailed into nothingness as Jack acknowledged the compliment with a brief, hard kiss. Her lips curved under his.

"As I was saying, the patent office requires a flash of *genius*."

"No problem," Jack responded, oozing confidence. "I'll be the genius. Any other criteria?"

"Yeah." Her smile changed to a full-fledged grin as she tightened her hold on the "genius" in her arms. "The invention has to be useful."

"That's a tough one." Jack fluffed the pillow behind her head, then rolled to his back and locked his fingers together behind his head as though in deep contemplation. "If the invention was a girl, we could make her do dishes."

"Boys don't do housework?" Samantha turned on her side and caught the mischievous gleam in his eyes. "They only take the trash out, right?"

"You wouldn't want a man to have dishpan hands, would you?" he goaded her.

Samantha growled and pretended to sink her teeth into the vulnerable flesh at the base of his neck. "I'd expect equal treatment for a boy or a girl."

She pulled herself on top of him. Jack grinned from ear to ear.

"That's what I'd expect," he whispered devilishly as he adjusted her legs on each side of his hips. "But I seem to recall another stipulation of the patent department.''

''What's that?'' her faked vampire bite switched to erotic nibbles as she prepared to conduct another experiment in the realm of desire.

''The inventor gets exclusive rights only if she does all the work.''

Playfully she bit his ear. ''Love, this is one experiment that takes joint effort for a novice.''

He settled her fully against himself, loving the whispered endearment. Jack reached for the nightstand and sighed, ''Never let it be said that Jack Martin shirked his responsibility. You'll have my enthusiastic cooperation.''

# Seven

The delicious smell of bacon, eggs and coffee teased Samantha awake. She glanced at the pillow beside hers. Jack had joked about a girl child having specified duties, but he obviously didn't practice what he preached. Knowing he was in the kitchen fixing breakfast pleased her. At the same time she wished she'd awakened earlier—in time to snuggle against his warmth.

"What we need," she muttered aloud, stretching, yawning, "is an automatic breakfast maker."

She sat up. Why not? There were stoves with timers that automatically started coffeepots. She cocked her head to one side as she contemplated the problem. Why not design an attachment to scramble eggs and fry bacon? What if...

Shaking her head, she ran her fingers through her tangled curls. Won't work, she mused. The coffeepot can be set up the previous night. Eggs and bacon have to be refrigerated. It was one thing to design an attachment, quite another to make a heater into a cooler that automatically reverted to a heater. Her mind flip-flopped as she visualized the concept.

Now wait a minute. Isn't that the principle behind a heat pump? Unconsciously she filled her mouth with air then tapped her cheek and expelled her breath.

Clothed for work in a three-piece navy blue suit, Jack entered the room and she gasped for more air. Without or with clothes, Jack Martin was, as Melissa would say, one hunk of a man.

"Morning," Jack said. He was holding a breakfast tray, and Samantha dug her heels into the water bed and pushed herself back against the headboard. As she did so, her hips arched provocatively under the satin coverlet. His dark eyes smiled appreciatively as he placed the tray on her lap.

"Don't stare," she said as she tried to keep some semblance of modesty by tucking the sheet under her arms. "I know I look like a mess in the morning."

His fingers followed the edge of the sheet. Sometimes touching the fabric, other times hopscotching along the swell of her breasts. "You look like a woman who's very satisfied with herself."

"You, too," Samantha said, including Jack in the compliment. The pointed tip of his tie fell from between his jacket lapels, landing in the shadowed valley of her breasts. She was tempted to use the stiff, silky fabric to pull him back into bed with her. "Thanks."

The unexpected simplicity of her expression of gratitude shook Jack. Only Serendipity Sam would consider thanking a man. Other women would be expecting gratitude, not giving it. God, he loved her uniqueness.

Put mentally off kilter by her response, he straightened, automatically murmuring politely, "You're welcome."

"I don't suppose I could convince you to play hooky today, could I?" she asked, wistfulness clearly evident in her voice.

"I haven't missed a day of work in years."

"You're kidding me. Everyone takes a mental health day once in a while or they go stir-crazy."

Jack laughed obligingly and straightened. A telltale flush crept from under his starched white collar and spread over his jaw. "O'Toole would probably have to close the plant down if I wasn't there to straw boss the operation."

"I realize you're reliable, but aren't you stretching the meaning of dedication?" She picked up the napkin and unwrapped the silverware. Eating breakfast in bed created problems that one didn't have when eating at a table. Here she didn't need to cover her lap with a napkin. She spread it under her chin.

"You won't want to play hooky when I tell you who I've arranged for you to have an appointment with." He paused, dangling the bait, waiting for her to snap it up.

The paper napkin slid off her chest and down toward her coffee cup. She grabbed it and pushed it back into place.

"Aren't you curious?"

The darned napkin began sliding again. "Yeah! How do you keep the napkin under your chin when you don't have a collar to tuck it into?" She grinned as she solved the problem. "Do you have any glue around here?"

"Sam! Stop worrying about spilling something on the sheets!"

Samantha shrugged, wadded the napkin and tossed it onto the tray. "I was just trying to be tidy. What did you say about an appointment for me?"

"I arranged for you to meet with the technical advisor about SAM trunks."

She hated to deflate his high spirits, but she had absolutely no intention of being hassled by a skeptic on Monday morning. "You'll have to cancel the appointment."

"Why?"

"Because yesterday you convinced me that O'Toole's would never consider marketing a competitive product."

In his eagerness to do something wonderful for Samantha, he'd totally forgotten the sage advice he'd given her. "Oh."

"I appreciate what you tried to do for me," she added to soften the blow, "but if you insist on punching the clock, would you mind dropping me off at the shop?"

"We'll have to hurry or I'll be late."

"What you mean is, eat and run. Thank goodness my work schedule isn't tied to the sweeping arm of the minute hand," she grumbled. She preferred to end their pleasant interlude with a slow leisurely breakfast. She sipped the black coffee. Her face screwed up in distaste. "No sugar?"

Jack glanced at his watch. He preferred arriving at work before the other employees. He hated being late.

"You eat while I get it."

She felt a rush of warm air as Jack hustled through the door and closed it. The first bite of eggs hadn't passed her lips when a brilliant thought struck her.

"That's it!" She snapped her fingers, then shifted the tray to the other side of the bed. "Every time someone goes in or out a door, the air currents move. Design a supersensitive sensor, electronically connect it to the light switch and . . . *zappo*! The lights turn on or off."

With the fork still in her hand, Sam rolled to her stomach. The tray shifted precariously as the water in the bed rolled. Sam didn't notice. Nothing registered but the hum of the bright idea going lickety-split through her brain. She used the fork to draw a sketch on the pillow.

From a course in basic electronics she'd taken, she knew most houses were similarly wired. She drew a square to represent a switch plate. All the contractor would have to do was. . . Lost in her thoughts, she drew a single line from the plate to a little niche that represented the door latch. She walked her fingers through the 'door.'

At the same moment her fingers were tramping over the pillowcase, Jack was returning from the kitchen. He hesitated before slowly opening the door. He expected Samantha to heave the contents of the tray at the door. To his way of thinking, Samantha had every right to pitch the entire tray in his face.

How boorish of him to put getting to work early ahead of reassuring her that their night together had been something special. He felt like a heel.

His mouth turning downward, he watched her silently pound the pillow with the handle of the fork. The tray swayed. Coffee sloshed from the cup onto her wadded napkin.

"Darn it!" Sam said, muttering to herself, as she often did when alone. "What an imbecilic idea. I should have known immediately that it wouldn't work."

Wasting mental energy on an impractical idea frustrated her. The only way her scheme would work was if a contractor built a windowless house with no heating or air-conditioning vents. Even a panting poodle would make the lights blink on and off. The police would be pounding on the door, thinking someone inside was sending emergency signals. "I'll have to start all over again!"

"I'm sorry," he said solemnly, unable to continue eavesdropping on her self-recriminations. He swiftly removed the tray to the bedside table. "Are you mad as hell at me?"

Samantha tossed the bedding downward as she swung her legs off the bed. "Mad? Why would I be mad?"

"I was inconsiderate. Guess I'm not used to having a beautiful woman stay with me."

She stared at Jack and wondered what in the world he was feeling guilty about. Sugar for her coffee wasn't *that* important.

"Forget it." Sam's eyes searched the carpet for her clothing. She spied it neatly folded on the clotheshorse in the corner of the room. Jack had not only prepared breakfast, he'd picked up after her. Inwardly she groaned. His "ready to conquer the business world" appearance made her acutely aware of her nudity. She grabbed her clothing and rushed into the adjoining bathroom, calling over her shoulder, "I'll be ready in just a minute."

The door slammed quicker than Jack could say, "I've changed my mind about going to work."

Sam's eyes rolled as she glanced from corner to corner of the bathroom. Sets of matching towels and washcloths broke the bathroom's sterility with bold, masculine earth tones. Monogrammed fingertip towels were neatly placed next to the sink. "He could film Mr. Clean commercials here," she whispered to herself as she noted the sparkling whiteness of the tiles and fixtures.

She glanced in the mirror. Smudges of mascara lined her eyes, which made her look like a blue-eyed raccoon. Automatically she reached for a washcloth, wet it, then stopped her hand in midair. Mascara-stained cloth. Jack wouldn't appreciate her ruining a set of his towels. She hung the washcloth on a brass rod. She leaned over and unrolled several squares of toilet paper. In her mother's picture-perfect home, she'd been provided with throw-away tissues. She scrubbed the mascara smudges, tossed the paper in the toilet and flushed it. So much for incriminating evidence, she thought.

Sam considered using Jack's toothbrush but decided against it. She might leave a telltale trace of toothpaste between the bristles. A bottle of antiseptic mouthwash caught her eye. Cupping her hand, she poured a small amount in her palm and sucked it into her mouth. For now, that would have to do, she thought.

Hurriedly she dressed. *Thank goodness I don't have to do this every morning,* she thought. There were advantages to living alone! Before she opened the door, she inspected the bathroom. Neat as a pin, she observed, silently congratulating herself.

"Ready," she said, charging toward the hallway, where Jack stood. Interpreting the clamped straightness of his lips to mean impatience, she said, "Come on, Jack. You're going to be late."

She literally ran from Jack's condo to his car.

"Can't get out of here fast enough," Jack muttered, locking the front door. Seconds later, inside the car, he watched Samantha smooth the fabric of her slightly wrinkled dress. He could tell from her nervous fidgeting that she resented his decision to rush off to work. He could almost see her compiling a lengthy list of reasons for not seeing him again. "You're thinking it won't work, aren't you?"

Lost in thought as she visualized a heat-sensitive sensor, Sam half listened. She assumed that he'd seen her drawing the circuitry on the pillow as well as heard her talking to herself. She felt slightly chagrined at being caught drawing a circuitry system on her pillow.

"No, it won't."

Sam mentally tested the flaws in an air-current device against those in a heat-sensitive device. Normal human body temperature was ninety-eight point six. People didn't keep their houses that hot. She wondered if dogs and cats had the same body temperature as people.

"Back to square one?"

She nodded. "Back to the drawing board."

As Jack turned the wheel, steering the car from the parking lot, he glanced at Samantha. She replied, but he'd detected a note of distraction in her voice. To make certain she was paying attention, he said, "You'd be insane to try to make it work, right?"

"Dumb idea to begin with."

Her replies made sense, but he still had the gut feeling that they weren't communicating. "I'd be insane to try to make it work, wouldn't I?"

Sam's brows furrowed. From her abstract sketches on the pillow, had Jack figured out what her current project was? What would O'Toole Life Preservers do with the designs for an automatic light switch? Jack was smart. Her eyes narrowed as she remembered Tom the

Thief. She trusted Jack, but she wasn't going to encourage him to dabble with her latest project.

"You can't make it work either."

She stared out the passenger's side window to avoid looking at him. They passed the street leading to the library. Right after Jack dropped her off, she'd call the librarian and find out the normal temperature of various household pets. Maybe she'd better call a veterinarian, she thought, as she added pythons to her mental list of pets. Would the temperature of a cold-blooded snake lying in the sun rise to ninety-eight point six degrees? The thought of having a snake as a pet made her shiver. Reflexively she rubbed her hands up and down her arms.

"Samantha, have you heard a word I've said?"

*Caught again,* Sam groaned to herself. She heard a familiar note of recrimination in his voice. She'd been listening to what he said. Well, almost listening, she amended silently, admitting her attention had been divided.

"Of course. You asked me if the design I sketched on your pillow would work. I said—"

"What design?"

"Don't play innocent. You apologized for sneaking a peek at my drawing, remember?" She felt a bit triumphant at being the catcher instead of the person caught. He must have been daydreaming, too.

"I apologized for being insensitive," Jack said, correcting her erroneous assumption.

"Insensitive? You? Don't be silly," she scoffed to cover her mistake. She'd done it again! Why, oh why, couldn't she keep her mind from straying when she was with a man? Men hated playing second fiddle to a vague idea. For a bright woman, she certainly felt dumb, repeatedly making the same mistake. Wouldn't she ever learn this simple lesson?

"Turn right at the next street. It's a shortcut to the shopping center."

Jack shot her a baleful glare and kept going straight. He knew exactly which way was the fastest. Hadn't he tested several routes from her place to his the day she'd refused to go out with him? He knew the quickest route to her shop, but he sure as hell didn't know the fastest way to her heart.

"I'm seldom . . . silly," he quietly rebuked her, then disproved it by asking a silly question. "Will I see you tonight?"

"Tonight?"

"You know, as in after work."

"I don't know."

"You don't know? *What* don't you know?"

"I don't know if I'll be finished with my work by five. I'll call you."

"You'll call *me*?" Jack sputtered. "Isn't that supposed to be my line?"

Samantha gave him a peculiar look. She'd heard the same tone of disbelief in the voices of her parents, her friends and the few men she'd dated. In effect, they were shouting, *You're not giving me top priority!*

Intuitively she knew explaining the electronic system in his car would be easier than making Jack understand what kept her motor purring. No one but another inventor could comprehend what made her different from other women.

The moment the car stopped, Sam opened the door, saying, "I'll call you."

Both of them knew she wouldn't.

"Samantha, we're going to talk this out. Now."

She waved her hand from side to side. "You'll be late for work. Bye."

Frustrated, Jack walloped the steering wheel with his palm. He checked his watch. He had sixteen minutes to get to work. It would take fourteen. Samantha had already entered her shop. What did she expect him to do? he fumed. Make a public fool of himself beating on the door and braying like a donkey for her to let him in?

Samantha strode to the back room. Talk wouldn't cure their problem any more than daydreaming had solved the light switch problem.

"He went to work," she muttered. "You go to work."

She pushed the curtain aside and went into the back room. Why did she feel like flinging herself on the cluttered sofa and bawling her eyes out of their sockets? She'd known she couldn't change. Hard as she tried, she knew Serendipity Sam couldn't sustain a relationship with a man.

Her hands on her temples, she dug her fingers through her hair. She clamped her eyelids shut. Black dots floated through grayness. Her lips tugged downward as the dark spots began to form into a likeness of Jack. Jack smiling. Laughing. Teasing. Serious. Satiated.

"Jack. Jack. Jack!" she mumbled, clenching her curls in an attempt to free herself from the mental images engraved in her consciousness. "Get the hell out of my shop!"

Her heartbeat accelerated when she heard a key being tapped against the front door. She'd credited Jack with being persistent, but not at the cost of being late to work.

Samantha peeked through the curtain. Jacob tapped his key again. She saw him frame his face with his hands to enable him to see into the dim interior of the shop.

"Sam! Open up!"

Relief mixed with disappointment. She'd wanted it to be Jack, but then again, she hadn't. Irked by her confused state of mind, she straightened her shoulders and strode to the door.

"What are you doing dressed up?" Jacob inquired, breezing in, flipping the overhead lights on.

Sam glanced at her rumpled clothing, embarrassed by the speculative gleam she saw in Jacob's eyes.

"Guess you worked after you came back from your parents' house yesterday, huh? Really, Sam. You could take time to change clothes. Those inventions of yours aren't going anywhere without you."

For once in their long friendship, Sam was grateful for Jacob's penchant for asking questions, answering them himself and then giving a long commentary. It gave her time to recover, to get her brain cells working.

"You're right on both counts," she agreed. "I should change clothes, and my inventions aren't going anywhere."

"Come on, Sam. You know what I meant. Don't be obtuse," Jacob chastised her as he unfolded a sheet of paper. "How're your parents?"

"Fine. They asked about you."

Jacob's blondish-brown eyebrows shot up. "Must have been your mother. Your dad practically booted me out of the front door. If you hadn't convinced me that your mother was the best cook in Houston, I'd have starved rather than face your father. Where he got the idea that florists were wimps, I'll never know."

Sam grinned. "Don't look at me. You're the one who raised your voice an octave and minced around the house."

"Purely self-defense, and you know it. Hangover from dealing with my own father, the roughneck. Our fathers both think a *real* man has oil under his fingernails."

"You're awful, Jacob," Sam protested, laughing. "Your dad hasn't worked on an oil rig in ten years."

"Yeah, but he still thinks men in the flower business are first cousins to produce men."

Missing the connection, Sam tilted her head quizzically.

"Nuts and fruits," he joked, patting her face as though to awaken her. "You're slow this morning Sam."

Sam couldn't argue the point.

"I heard an interesting rumor via the drapery shop," Jacob continued. He scratched his smooth jaw as though trying to remember. "Melissa said something about a gorgeous hunk and scrumptious buns. At first, I thought Melissa was drooling over a tenderloin at the store."

Watching Jacob roll his tongue around in his cheek, Sam could almost see his ears perk up as he waited expectantly for her reply. "You know how Melissa exaggerates," Samantha said dismissively.

"I watered down her version. Jack Martin, huh? Eons ago I went to school with a guy named Jonathan Martin. Kids called him Jack. Well built, dark haired, athletic, but the honor roll type. Won the senior class presidency by sheer persistence."

"He's from Dallas. Can't be the same Jack Martin."

Jacob laughed with delight. "Must be. I grew up in Plano, Texas. Lived with my mother while Dad climbed oil rigs all over the world." He scratched his smoothly shaven jaw reflectively. "Well, I'll be damned. You and Jack Martin. Who'd believe—"

"Don't believe *anything* Melissa told you."

"She said you took him to your folks' for dinner."

It was Samantha's turn to smile. "Mom served him peanut-butter-glazed ham. He ate it like it was good."

"Didn't you ever eat ham-and-peanut-butter sandwiches? When I was a kid, I traded my home-made pie for a big, thick sandwich."

"Disgusting," Sam jibed. "You're making that up, just like you're making up the unlikely claim that you know the same Jack Martin that I know."

"Do the descriptions match?"

"Well, uh, tall, dark and handsome describes half the men in Houston."

Jacob's grin broadened. "Handsome? Did I say handsome?"

Avoiding his verbal trap, she poked Jacob in the ribs good-naturedly and said, "Melissa's description."

Jacob frowned, then visibly winced. "I can't picture Melissa with Jack. Next time you see him, have him drop by the floral shop. I'd love to talk over old times. Find out what he's up to lately."

Seeing Sam blush for the first time since he'd met her, he thrust the wrinkled paper in his hand toward her. "Put your brain in gear and take a look at this."

Her cheeks tingling hotly, Sam glanced at the paper in hopes that Jacob would forget about Jack Martin. She certainly wasn't going to encourage the two of them to get together to cuss and discuss her.

"Cartoons?" she asked as she perused a crude drawing of a Texas Aggie in a scruffy football uniform, who was carrying a bouquet of summer flowers and a football that had Aggies Love Flowers written across the laces.

"What do you think, Sam? Father's Day is the only holiday that's slow in the flower business." He pointed to the ball. "I want it to wave back and forth like the ole boy is getting ready to throw a touchdown pass. I think it's great," he enthused. "Can you muster up a mechanical marvel if I provide the mannequin?"

"Whoa! Which question do you want answered first?"

Jacob glanced over his shoulder in time to see Melissa pass by the Fixit Shop. His homely face changed as he grinned devilishly. He casually looped his arm around Sam's shoulder, tightened his hold and boldly dipped her backward. A glint of teasing innuendo lit his green eyes. "Skip the one asking for your opinion. Get to the can you do it."

"If only our fathers could see us now," Samantha chuckled, hanging on for dear life. She found herself standing upright immediately.

"Forget them." He shook the paper in her face. "I'd rather encounter a football field full of Dallas Cowboys than have your dad behind me at a church altar. Can you imagine what he'd bellow when the minister asked, 'Does anyone object to this marriage?' I'm no wimp, but I'm not that brave." With a wink he added, "I seem to recall Jack Martin was a helluva quarterback."

For a fraction of a second, Samantha pictured herself dressed in a frothy wedding dress. But it wasn't Jacob she envisioned beside her. The Chantilly lace bubbling from a sheer cuff rested on the dark sleeve of Jack Martin. Mentally, she turned around, seeking her father's reaction. Her dad beamed his approval while her mother dabbed at the tears of happiness slipping down her cheeks.

Shaking her shoulder and snapping his fingers, Jacob shattered the image.

"Thinking about a new project?" Jacob asked, knowing how her mind wandered to the back of the shop when she felt inspired. "I need you to work on this. Did you get your water and trash pickup bills? I'll pay yours, if you'll get the football star ready by this weekend. Fair?"

Dazed, Sam nodded her head. Like most women, she'd conjured a wedding scene before but never in such vivid detail. She could almost smell the orange blossoms.

"Sam! Was that a yes?"

"No!" she said, rebelling against the idea of marriage. "I can't!"

"You're mad about me not making it to Astro Hall, aren't you? I thought you'd be over that by now. I'll send you one of my best floral arrangements. Sam, I don't have time to get down on my knees and grovel. I'm up to my arms in orange blossoms and hurricane lamps for Gail Kincaid's wedding. Be a sweetheart, would you?"

During Jacob's fast-paced analysis of her rejection, Sam realized she'd spoken her words aloud. Smiling wanly, she said, "Friday soon enough?"

"Thanks, Sam. You're a doll!" He rushed to the door, as though certain she'd change her mind if he didn't make a fast exit. "I'll call you later in the week."

Crumpling the drawing in her hand, Sam gave a groan of despair. Along with her other bad habits, she'd acquired a new one since meeting Jack Martin. Now her active imagination included mechanical drawing and . . . weddings.

A shiver raced down her spine. Samantha wrapped her arms across her chest. She had to physically hold herself together or the self-image she'd constructed of being a self-sufficient, independent woman would explode into a zillion pieces.

The delicate underside of her wrist brushed against the fullness of her breast as she raised her hand to her brow. Now that her sleeping femininity had been awakened by Jack's touch, it seemed unwilling to return to its previous dormant state.

Much as she wanted to ignore the fact that she was a woman with normal physical urges, she couldn't. By closing her eyes and allowing herself to relax, Samantha knew she could recall each moment of the previous night. Her traitorous body had taken notes far more carefully that those she entered in her inventor's log.

Her lips curved into a wry smile. A woman's body and an inventor's brain. What a mismatch.

*Serendipity Sam and the class president,* she derided herself. *What a joke.*

Only Samantha wasn't laughing.

*So what are you going to do about it?* Absentmindedly she tossed the wad of paper in her hand into the air. She sought an easy, logical solution but found only a ludicrous idea.

"Brain transplant. Better yet, a spare brain that matches my body. One I could insert when Jack is around and take out when I'm here to work. One that wouldn't detour on a creative binge while lying on a man's pillow.''

She hurled the scrap of paper across the room. Jacob's drawing bounced off the curtain separating the two rooms and fell to the floor. Grimacing at her futile gesture, she followed the direction of the missile. She parted the curtain as she stooped to retrieve the paper. Dust balls, she noted, picking up the paper and the lint. She slowly raised her eyes and suddenly saw the room through Jack's eyes.

The contrast between Jack's condo and her living quarters startled her. No wonder he didn't want to sit down while he ate his sandwich, she thought, glancing toward the corner where she'd stashed the broom and dustpan.

Her off-gray walls contrasted shabbily with the pristine whiteness of the tiles in his bathroom. Her clutter compared unfavorably with his orderliness. She couldn't remember the last time she'd done what her mother called spring cleaning.

"I'm not going to clean the shop to impress Jack," she muttered mulishly. "I'm doing it for myself."

# Eight

—

$F$riday night, Jack parked his car in the far, dark corner of Sam's parking lot. He'd decided early in the week that sitting at home by the telephone was a waste of time. Pride kept Jack from calling her but not from haunting the place she worked. He'd parked his car in the El Camino Shopping Center parking lot so often that he was certain the postman would start delivering his mail there.

To pass the time, he'd counted light standards, panes of plate glass and cars. And lame excuses.

Monday, after he'd dropped Sam at the shop, he flattered himself into believing their little tiff was merely the result of discovering how wonderful they were together. A man who prided himself on earning every nickel of his paycheck, he was appalled to find himself daydreaming about her at work and wishing he'd played hooky after all.

By late afternoon, the daydreams turned to erotic fantasies that included sexy black silk hosiery held up by a fragile lacy garter belt that matched a cob-web sheer bra. His mouth watered as his taste buds recalled the taste of passion on her lips. The sensitive pads of his fingertips remembered the silkiness of her skin, her hair. Because of the explicit sensuality of his fantasy, he had to stay behind his desk to avoid embarrassing himself in front of his secretary.

Yes indeed, he'd felt certain that within twenty-four hours she'd call.

Tuesday, he'd justified being in the parking lot by telling himself he needed the fresh air. Idly sitting in his car munching on junk food hardly qualified, but he needed an excuse.

In a moment of supreme weakness, he'd considered purchasing new drapes. Melissa would know why Sam's shop had been shut down for two days. He abandoned the thought when he remembered how Melissa's eyes had mentally devoured him the night Sam had introduced them.

Midweek, his self-assurance began to wane. Samantha said she'd call. Why hadn't she? Not leaving anything to chance, he called the telephone company to make certain her phone was connected and working properly. It was. She should have called but hadn't. How dare she spend the night with him, then casually forget to telephone! The least she could have done was send a rejection letter!

Righteous indignation changed to suppressed anger on Thursday. And tonight, Friday, he'd decided to take action. His troubled, dark eyes willed Sam to walk through her door. The Closed sign, slightly askew, remained on the Fixit Shop window. Only the glimmer of light filtering from the back room reassured him that she was in there.

*Doing what?* he silently demanded, thoroughly concerned. There had to be some logical reason for her not to have called. Something must have happened to her, he concluded in an attempt to save the last shreds of his pride. Since he cared about her, it was his responsibility to make certain she wasn't sick or injured, and unable to get to the phone, waiting for someone to rescue her.

Jack worried his lower lip between his teeth. In five days his pride had slipped to an all-time low.

From the passenger seat he picked up the box of chocolates he'd bought earlier and the toaster he'd broken with a screwdriver. Candy made sick people feel better, didn't it? He silently groaned at the implausible excuse he'd made up for her not calling. Knowing Sam she'd cast the candy aside and be thrilled with the broken toaster!

With one last glance in the rearview mirror to make certain his tie was straight and his hair neatly combed, he opened the car door. His damp hands left fingerprints on the polished door handle. He used his handkerchief to wipe the thin sheen of perspiration from his hands, his forehead, his upper lip. Maybe, he mused wryly, I should eat the candy.

His stride shortened the closer he came to the Fixit Shop. He dawdled, pretending to window-shop. A seven-foot mannequin waving a football drew his attention. Flowers? Why not, he decided, entering the florist's shop.

The man behind the counter twisting green tape around a wire looked vaguely familiar to Jack. He shrugged, dismissing the thought that perhaps he knew him. He'd probably seen the florist a dozen times while he'd been watching for Samantha.

"Can I help you?" Jacob raised his eyes. "Jack? Jack Martin? Why you devil! Sam mentioned—no, it was Melissa who mentioned meeting you." Jacob circled the counter, hand extended. "Jacob Klein, Plano, class of seventy!"

Jack set the candy and toaster on the counter. He pumped Jacob's hand as though they were long lost blood brothers. His dark eyes widened as he connected Jacob with the floral shop. "Good to see you. Last time I heard anything about you . . ."

"You heard I'd followed my father's footsteps to the North Atlantic oil rigs?" Jacob laughed, not the least bit discomforted. "I get seasick, homesick and sick of Texas tea. Bad combination for a roughneck. What have you been doing with yourself?"

"I'm with O'Toole Life Preservers . . . life jackets."

"Oh, yeah? I guess that's how you met Sam. Sweet girl, Sam," Jacob added, testing the waters. He glanced pointedly at the toaster. "For her?"

Jack grinned, somewhat abashed at resorting to candy and a broken appliance to woo a woman. "Not girl, woman," he corrected, nodding his head.

"Small world," Jacob said, returning the grin. "Lilacs are out of season. They're her favorite. How about a nice bouquet of forget-me-nots?"

Jack heard the note of glee in Jacob's voice. "Appropriate choice. You must know her well."

Jacob crossed to a refrigerated display case, slid the glass to the side and removed a nosegay of delicate flowers. "I know she forgets to eat, forgets to pay bills, forgets to do almost everything except go to her parents' for dinner on Sunday." He held the bouquet forward for Jack's inspection. "You want me to deliver these?"

Tempted to soften Samantha with flowers before he arrived on her doorstep, he started to agree.

"Never mind. I can't deliver them," Jacob said, typically answering his own question.

Pointing toward the figurine of Mercury, then touching the wings on the god's feet, Jack asked, "Don't you deliver?"

"Is the sign still on her door?"

"Yes, but—"

"In that case, it wouldn't do any good. She won't open the door. Must be working on something important."

"It's been there all week. What's she doing? Repairing every blender, microwave and child's toy in Houston?" His exasperation and frustration dripped between each item listed.

"What do *inventors* usually do? Invent things! It isn't unusual for Sam to lock herself in and let the world follow it's own course while she follows hers."

Hiking his slacks, Jack's eyes narrowed as he contemplated Jacob's smug, I-know-her-better-than-you-do look. "The world is about to come to a screeching halt. I'm going to the Fixit Shop and beat on the door until she opens it."

"Persistent as ever," Jacob muttered with a deep sigh.

"Nothing wrong with persistence, is there?"

Biting his tongue, Jacob shrugged. He knew good and well what would happen when Jack started banging on the window. A devilish look panned across Jacob's homely features. But for the sake of the old alma mater, he warned, "I wouldn't if I were you."

"Don't put the flowers back in the case. I'll be back . . . with Samantha."

Jacob held his breath as he watched Jack charge between the potted plants. The subtle fragrance of the nosegay tickled his nose but not nearly as much as the thought of Sam's burglar alarm going off tickled his sense of humor. Admittedly it was ornery of him not to tell Jack about the lion. He really should have been more explicit with his warning. Recalling a movie he'd recently seen called *The Revenge of The Nerds*, he grinned. Jacob didn't consider himself a stereotype nerd, nor Jack a typical class president, but he couldn't help the teeny ripple of pleasure he felt knowing that Sam was giving Jack a conniption fit. He strummed his fingers on the counter, waiting for Jack to barge through the front door.

Wild-eyed, Jack flung himself through the door of the flower shop. "My God, Jacob, there's a lion in Samantha's shop. My banging on the window must have enraged it. We've got to get in there!"

"I didn't see a lion the last time I was there," Jacob replied with unperturbed innocence.

"Give me the phone. I'm going to call the cops! Have you got a hatchet to break the plate glass?"

Jacob tried to restrain his laughter. It defied concealment. He tossed his head back and roared. "That's a recording! Sam's burglar alarm. Jar the window and you hear a tape recording of a lion during mating season."

"Why the hell would she do that? I lost ten years of my life thinking she'd been—" He swallowed the fear that had blocked his throat.

"Eaten? Sam's a tough cookie. Any lion with a healthy respect for his teeth wouldn't touch her."

"Not funny, Jacob." Jack's hand shook as he picked up the chocolates. "Is there another way into her shop?"

"Today's Friday. If you'll wait until Saturday, I'm certain she'll surface."

"What's special about Saturday?"

"Sunday she eats dinner at her parents'."

Jack felt as though he was stuck in a revolving door and wasn't getting anywhere. "What the hell does eating with her parents on Sunday have to do with her coming up for air on Saturday?"

"Simple. She loves them. Sam told me the one time her mother raised holy Cain was when she arrived with dark circles under her eyes. She needs twenty-four hours to put herself back together so her mother won't be upset."

"That's simple?" Jack muttered sarcastically. "Now why didn't I think of that reason?"

"Because you don't understand what makes her tick."

A flash of acute jealousy flattened Jack's lips against his teeth. "And you do?"

"Heavens, no," Jacob chuckled. "I'm quoting her. She doesn't make a bit of sense to me, either."

"Well, mister I've waited long enough. You've just met the clock maker. I'm going to discover what makes her tick if it takes me the next hundred years!"

"So speaks a man in love," Jacob replied, wondering what sort of incomprehensible mechanics were behind Melissa's ticking. He'd given up on winning her with candy and flowers. Like an overwound clock, she literally needed to be taken apart.

"Love?" Of all the emotions Jack had felt this week, he wasn't certain love was one of them.

Jacob made a tsking noise and shook his head. "You haven't changed one iota. Just the other day I was telling Sam how you got elected as class president through perseverance." He chuckled, thinking out loud, "Wonder if it'll work with Sam? Charisma versus creative. Interesting." He handed Jack the nosegay. "Forget-me-nots and Texas bluebonnets. Both flowers grow wild in their own habitat but suffer from transplant shock in unfamiliar environments. Same color but unsuitable for an arrangement."

"Thanks for the vote of confidence. I'll bet you voted for George for class president, didn't you?"

"As a matter of fact, I didn't. The odds were against you then and now, but I know a winner when I see one." He gestured over his shoulder with his thumb. "Try the door in the alley. She's been scurrying in and out of it all week. Sometimes she forgets to lock it when she's on a creative binge."

"Thanks, Jacob." He picked up the box of chocolates, tucking it under his arm.

"Be careful. She isn't hospitable to uninvited guests."

Jack nodded as he wove his way between plastic buckets filled with fresh flowers. With Samantha, he was slowly learning to expect the unexpected.

Moments later, he cautiously tested the knob on her back door. He heard the latch open. With the sound of a lion's roar still in his ears, he carefully pushed inward. He wouldn't put it past Samantha to rig some sort of disaster to befall any feckless character who mistakenly entered her domain without permission. He glanced to make certain he wasn't walking under a booby trap, then gave a small sigh of relief. No bucket of water.

His dark eyes rounded in surprise. Her living area was immaculate. The smell of fresh paint and the scent of pine flared his nostrils. His heart did a backward somersault when he saw Samantha hunched over the workbench, precariously close to falling from her perch on a high stool. Barely making a sound, he dropped the flowers on the freshly made sofa bed and moved toward her. As though she were a precious child, he gently lifted her from the stool.

"What am I going to do with you?" he whispered against the soft curls at the crown of her head.

She didn't stir.

Jack lowered her to the bed. Her mouth moved, parting. Unable to resist her allure, he brushed her lips with his own. With a small sigh, and a slight smile, Samantha curled the pillow in her arms.

For long minutes he allowed himself the pleasure of watching Samantha sleep. Her ragged, paint-splattered cutoff jeans gave him unrestricted view of her shapely legs. Perfectly proportioned, he thought appreciatively. One leg was tucked up toward her chest. His eyes followed the same path to the faded T-shirt. It had been washed so much that the lettering on the front wasn't readable.

His throat constricted as he realized she wasn't wearing a bra. The threadbare cotton fabric molded against her roundness. His eyes turned to black as they lingered on the contrasting darkness of her nipples. Another woman might feign the seductive pose, but he knew Samantha was innocent of deception.

Desire stirred within him.

The room seemed warmer. He removed his jacket and tie, draping them over a straight-backed chair. Conscious of the noise his shoes were making on the bare floor, he bent down and untied them, Out of habit, he placed his shoes at the foot of the bed. As though his fingers had a will of their own, they nimbly unbuttoned his shirt to the waist.

"Jack . . ."

In her sleep, she'd murmured his name. The intimate hushed call made his heart skip a beat. He unbuckled his belt.

Samantha's dream followed the same uninhibited path it had taken the past four nights. Jack arrived, his dark eyes stormy, ready to give her holy hell for not calling. He'd crashed through the door like a summer squall. Then, when he saw the changes she'd made, he smiled. The dream glowed with the muted hues of the rainbow.

In her sleep, she echoed his smile, called his name as she opened her arms. "No," she wasn't angry with him. "No," she hadn't called, but she hadn't called because she wanted to surprise him.

His hand stopped on the zipper beneath the fly of his slacks. *No?* Had he heard her say, "No"?

Unaware Jack had deciphered the first word in her mutterings, in her dream she wrapped her arms around his broad shoulders and rubbed her face against his shirt front, anticipating . . ."

Jack watched her hug the pillow. Her cheek rubbed the pillowcase.

Invitation coupled with rejection, he thought, analyzing her dream.

He brushed his hand down the light switch. Blackness shrouded the small room. Her husky contradiction had brought the room back into focus. The paint odor was heavy and it was difficult to breathe. Jack folded his arms across his chest and leaned back against the wall. A mild expletive silently vented his frustration.

"She's a bundle of contradictions," he groaned aloud. Softly calling his name contradicted the harsh finality of the word "no." Her guileless innocence contradicted her womanly passion. She was half child, half seductive temptress. She exemplified the logical precision of a research scientist while contradicting herself by her illogical, scatterbrained life-style.

The memory of holding Samantha in his arms, of sharing an intimacy as deep any two people could experience, kept him from silently slipping into the darkness outside. He shook his head. He couldn't return to his empty bed. Knowing she wouldn't be there made it seem wider, emptier, colder. He wasn't certain he could face another night of loneliness.

Funny, he thought, he'd never considered himself lonely until he'd met Samantha. Alone, self-sufficient, goal oriented, but never, never lonely.

Now what? he asked himself, knowing he was in over his head. His self-confidence teetered. What had happened to his belief that he could get anything he wanted by working for it? He wanted Samantha. What could he do to get her?

*Think!* He specialized in making plans, in analysis, in plotting a course, working out the kinks and following through until he reached his goal. Excluding the last phase, wasn't that what Samantha did, too?

His strengths were her weaknesses. His steadiness complemented her flightiness. His single-mindedness would keep her from shooting off in twenty different directions. His marketing skills could make her dreams become a reality.

Jack rejected Jacob's flower theory.

Together he and Sam were better than when separated.

"Who's there?" Samantha asked sleepily.

"Me—" Jack moved to the side of the sofa bed "—Jack."

"How long have you been here?" She covered her mouth as she yawned.

"Not long. I got worried when I didn't hear from you this week."

Samantha smiled, remembering how pleased she was with herself when she'd moved the last piece of furniture back into place. "I've been busy."

"Painting?"

"Cleaning, building shelves, organizing." She propped herself up on one elbow, then leaned back to see Jack's face. "You're towering over me. Why don't you sit down? Or better yet, lie down."

Jack watched her move back, making room for him beside her. A second invitation wasn't necessary.

The flimsy mattress shifted under his weight and Samantha rolled against him. In her half-awake state, she hadn't noticed before that he was only wearing his trousers. She nuzzled the springy hair on his chest. "Where were we?"

"You were telling me what you've been doing all week." He wedged his hand under the slight curve of her waist and drew her more fully across him.

"Working every minute," she sighed. Her aching muscles, unaccustomed to physical labor, protested against any abrupt movements. "Did you take a look at the shop?"

"Uh-uh." He rolled a curl around his forefinger. Pure luxury, he thought, feeling its silky fineness with his thumb. At the tip he felt a small dot of paint. "You have paint in your hair."

"Hmmm. If you'd been patient and waited for my call, I'd have been clean, clothed and perfumed."

"I'm not complaining."

Lazily Samantha circled his flat male nipple with her fingers. She wondered if her touching him caused the same delicious sensations that she felt when he touched her breasts. She lightly kissed the tip. It puckered in response. The same way hers did. His quick intake of air answered her question.

"Still tired?" Jack asked, doing his best to control the activity below his open belt buckle, but having little success.

"A little."

Jack clamped his eyes shut as the tiny serrations of her upper teeth grazed the tight bud between her lips. "Want me to go?"

"Would you?" Samantha teased, rocking against him.

"I'd give it a hell of a try. I have enough willpower left to crawl to the door."

"You'd get the knees of your slacks dirty. She flicked his nipple with her tongue.

"Not on this floor. I could eat off of it." He felt her lips curve into a satisfied smile.

"Love it, don't you?"

"If you mean what you're doing, and not the floor, yes." He groaned his appreciation as he pulled her completely on top of himself. "Are you going to have your way with me?" He paused. "I hope."

Knowing his penchant for cleanliness, she raised herself to slide off the side of the bed. "I need a shower. I smell like a horse."

"I'm a sucker for pine scent and paint. Stay where you are." He raised the hem of her shirt, swiftly pulled it over her head and tossed it toward the chair. He cupped her breasts, weighing them, anticipating their taste. His thumbs rotated in opposite directions over her nipples. Lifting his head, he savored one, then the other, as he moved backward until he leaned against the cushions of the sofa with Samantha straddling his hips.

"We could take a shower together," she suggested.

"Later." he arched his hips, setting her firmly against him. "Make love with me."

His fingers made quick work of her jeans' snap and zipper. For a bare second, when his hand splayed the fabric and he discovered she wasn't wearing any underclothes, she felt embarrassed. She started to explain.

His mouth covered hers. His tongue flickered inside her sweetness as his fingers strummed against her, inside her. Explanation fled; sensation precluded thought.

Her lips wildly raced over his face, hot and moist, rough and ruthless. His long, lithe body bucked under hers, setting a frantic need coursing through her. To keep her balance, she grabbed the back of the sofa. Detecting her imbalance, he slowed the rocking motion, letting her set the pace.

"Closer. More," she gasped, suddenly hating the barrier of clothing between them. "Help me."

She swung one leg to the side. Attuned to her every need, Jack removed her cutoffs and shed his slacks and underwear. Samantha groaned as she reclaimed his hips with her legs, felt the blast of his heat at the juncture of her thighs. The hard firmness of him pressed against her. So good. So right. No man had ever wanted her like this. Free. Flying. Weightless.

Power surged through her. Her mind skyrocketed in a thousand unexplored directions. When they'd made love before, she'd gloried in the feeling of equality. Although she was on her knees, she dominated. Or, she wondered fleetingly was this another form of equality? She'd pleased him by laboriously straightening the shop, and now, he pleased her.

She studied his face, searching for an answer. One hand continued to steady her, but the other skimmed across her breasts, her neck, her hair. His eyes closed in concentration. His lips moved soundlessly. She moved her hands from the sofa to rest on either side of his head on the pillow. Leaning close, she brushed her nipples over his chest. She heard his tortured words of desire, of need, of longing.

Jack prolonged his last upward thrust as he felt her pulse around him. He clung to her hips, then as she collapsed across his chest, turned her until she was beneath him. Control, he thought, silently congratulating himself for refusing the temptation to plunge inside her warmth and instantly satisfy himself.

Limply, lifelessly, Samantha draped her arms around his neck. Her eyes fluttered as the tip of his tongue leisurely traced her love-swollen lips. His hips slowly moved, bringing her down from the ultimate pinnacle of love. A smile of delight curved her lips.

"You know this isn't possible, don't you?" she whispered.

"Nothing's impossible between us." He withdrew, then inch by inch let her feel his strength. "I've missed you."

"I've read that abstinence has the opposite effect on men."

"Not when they have reasons for testing their control."

"Reason? I lost all sense of reason long, long minutes ago." Her hips rolled. She loved the feel of his hair-peppered skin against her.

"I want you to remember this night," he whispered hoarsely. The control he'd boasted of began slipping. He tried to concentrate on anything other than how she fit him like a sleek, silken glove. The subtle fragrance of the nosegay next to her head on the pillow provided him with a short reprieve. "To forget-me-not," he whispered, adding in his last moment of sanity as she arched against him, "to remember me."

# Nine

I'm impressed," Jack said, strolling through the shop, sipping his morning coffee.

Samantha's chest swelled. She pointed from one wall to the other. "See. I put the household repairs on this side, the toys over there. I'm displaying a few of my inventions in the front window. What better place to sell them than from my own shop?"

"The pictures of the great inventions that you've hung on the wall add a nice touch." He crossed the floor to the window. In apple-pie order, she'd displayed the SAM trunks on one side and a myriad of household inventions on the other. He picked up the pair of trunks he'd worn the first night they'd met. "I'll buy these if you'll autograph them."

"Any place special you'd like to have my signature? Left or right cheek?"

Jack sputtered into his coffee at her remark and the audacious way her eyebrows arched. He pretended to examine the fabric. He didn't need her autograph to identify the indelible brand she'd put on him.

In the responsibility-free life-style Samantha had created for herself, Jack felt certain Sam wanted a no-strings-attached relationship. One word about permanence of any sort and she'd kick him right out the front door. He had to insinuate himself into her life, gradually making her realize that she couldn't exist without him.

Good plan, he thought. And now for the execution. "Have you seen those little tags mothers sew on their kids' clothes when they send them off to college? Put one with your company name and address on the swimsuits."

"Hopefully the elastic in the waistband will keep the wearer from losing them. I don't plan on running a lost and found department in the Fixit Shop."

"No, honey, that's not what the tags are for. They're for free advertising. You might get enough word-of-mouth advertising to start a mail-order business."

Samantha sidled up next to him. "You're the only male I want to order," she teased. She looped her arms around his neck.

"You want a male you can order around?" he asked, twisting her words as agilely as she had twisted his.

"No," she whispered against his throat. "I don't take orders and I don't give them. I hate being told what to do."

Jack rubbed her nape with both thumbs. "I'm not bossing you. Would a few helpful hints insult you?"

"Such as?" Samantha put her hands on his shoulders and looked him straight in the eye.

"Well, now that you've asked me—"

"I'm not *real* certain I have, but go ahead anyway."

He brushed his lips across hers to erase the slightly defiant pout he saw. "After I saw your shop, I realized how much money I've been wasting by pitching small appliances that didn't work properly. Do you know how much a new blender costs?"

"I've never bought one."

"One that will last longer than the limited guaranteewill cost around thirty dollars. What did you charge to fix that one?"

"Nothing. I traded services."

"Isn't that like the one you fixed for the manager of the grocery store?"

"Yeah? So? He gave me the coffee you're drinking."

"What's the owner of that blender going to trade?"

"He's a plumber. If my pipes freeze next winter, he'll fix them for free."

"Have your pipes ever frozen?"

That wicked eyebrow arched again. "They might," she said, laughing.

"Not with me around to thaw them," Jack muttered, unable to resist insinuating that he'd still be in her life come wintertime. Straight-faced, he asked, "Have you ever considered charging for your services?"

"I'm into bartering. Tit for tat," she replied naughtily, poking him in the chest.

"You'll wind up being the runt of the litter if you don't put a cash register back there and use it." He caught her shoulders as she spun away from him. "I'm sorry, Samantha. I don't want to hurt you. But it bothers me to see you scrimping and saving to finance your inventions when you should be making a mint off this side business. It bugs me to see you let strangers off the street take advantage of you."

Samantha realized he was being practical. Constructive criticism from a successful businessman should be heeded.

She glanced at the commercial mixmaster on the shelf next to the blender. The baker down the street owned it. Mentally she tabulated the number of day-old cakes, donuts and buns she'd eaten. Lemon meringue pie and blackberry cobbler were the desserts she preferred. The only time her sweet tooth was satisfied was when she went to her mother's house.

"How much is that mixmaster?" she asked.

"Looks expensive. A hundred. Maybe more."

"And he'd throw it away if I didn't fix it?"

"Probably."

"What about that food processor?"

The man who operated the cleaners had brought it in. Recalling the limited contents of her closet, she realized trading for a thirty percent discount was foolish. Zero couldn't be discounted. She hadn't taken anything to the cleaners in months.

"Why don't I bring a Wilson's catalog over here? You'll be able to figure out who paid what."

"Could you locate a tool catalog? I repair everything from hole hogs to copper choppers."

"I'll get one from a small equipment supply house."

"While you're there, ask them if they'd be interested in sending me some of their business. Contractors are always griping about equipment being on the distributor's workshop table."

Her mind spun at the prospect of transforming a peanut-butter-and-jelly income into a steak-and-baked-potatoes fortune. She'd display signs on the repaired equipment. Letting the customer know how much he paid initially for the item and showing how reasonable her rate to repair it was.

Why not clean the appliances too? Elbow grease and a mild cleaner would make them sparkle like new. Samantha wondered how much she should charge.

Her days of working for nothing had ended.

"Samantha?" Jack waved his hand in front of her eyes. "Your mind is wandering again."

"Something you'll have to get used to if you're going to put up with me," she warned softly.

"We'd avoid misunderstandings if you'd share your thoughts."

"I thought men liked mysterious women," she teased.

"Honey, you don't have a thing to worry about on that score. You're as complicated as the most sophisticated piece of machinery in here." He inched her forward until their thighs, hips and waists touched. "I want to be more than physically close to you. Your mind is as intriguing as your delectable body."

A shaft of pleasure pulsed through Samantha. Most men couldn't care less what was between her ears. Often she'd wondered if she'd have been more popular if that space had been completely devoid of gray matter.

She rested her cheek on his shirt front. Jack was different. She sighed, indicating her state of contentment.

"I was thinking about making small signs showing how much the customer saved by bringing his broken equipment to the Fixit Shop."

"Sound business practice. Are you up for one more little suggestion?"

Hoping Jack's thoughts were drifting in the same directions hers were—toward the rumpled bed in the back room—she nodded her head agreeably.

"Post the hours you're open for business on the front door and stick to them religiously."

Samantha groaned her disappointment. "I hate being hemmed into a work schedule. Stifles my creativity."

"But it brings in customers. Think about the poor man or woman who drives out of their way to drop off something to be fixed. They get here and that damned closed sign greets them. After a few such trips, they pitch the broken appliance and swear never to come back."

"Good business practice," she grumbled, seeing his logic, but dreading the thought of people invading those unscheduled hours of privacy she needed to work on her projects.

"You don't have to be open from nine to five. Just make certain that when you say you're going to be open, you are. When is the shopping center most active?"

"Who knows?" And who cares, she thought. "I don't have time to count people as they pass the front of the store."

"I'll ask Jacob. He'll know. Keep the shop open during those hours."

"The lion roars on Saturday. People beat on the door all day and set off my burglar alarm," she explained. She moved out of his arms and crossed to the door. If she was going to restructure her work day, she might as well start immediately. It is Saturday, isn't it? she thought, not too certain what day of the week it was.

"Your burglar alarm scared me witless last night. I thought you'd been devoured."

Sam grinned as she unlocked the door. "Very effective device. Better than the snarling Doberman that I tried to sell to the burglar alarm manufacturers. Actually I thought it was a superneat gadget. When the window pane vibrated, it activated two glowing green eyes, and at the same time, the barking began. Much better than a sign that says beware of dog, don't you think?"

"Where in the world do you come up with these ideas?" Jack said with a chuckle, then picked up his tepid coffee and took a sip. Automatically he grimaced his distaste.

"From people like you." She pointed to the cup he'd set on the table. "First, I find a need. You dislike cold coffee, right?"

Jack nodded, following her train of thought.

"How many half cups of coffee do you throw away?"

"Several."

"Wasteful." She flipped over the sign on the door. "Why couldn't some creative genius invent a small energy source to put in the bottom of the mug to keep the coffee hot?"

"I suppose you have a patent on such a cup?"

Sam shrugged. "I'll admit to fiddling around with the idea, but I haven't perfected anything. Once I come up with an idea, I have to make it practical. That's the tough part."

"What's difficult about implanting a small electrical unit in the bottom of the cup?"

"Are you going to fight a plug and a wire every time you take a sip?" She shook her head. "Uh-uh. You want a cup that will look and feel like a regular cup but one that will keep your coffee hot."

"Did you invent one?"

"Let's say I solved that problem but created another one."

"How? What?"

"My two favorite questions," she quipped, happy that Jack took an interest in her work. "I wrapped the cup with a thin, lightweight wire. The scalding hot coffee heated the wire, which stayed hot longer than the liquid inside the cup."

"And...?"

"I burned my bottom lip."

"Don't make the wire come up to the rim," Jack suggested, getting into the swing of curing the defect in her invention.

"That's exactly what I did." She walked to the counter and picked up a dust cloth. After spending five long days cleaning and painting, she wasn't going to let a speck of dusk mar her efforts. "Then I came to problem two: washing the cup. Inexpensive wire rusts. Have you any idea how expensive a cup lined with gold wire would cost?"

"Find a manufacturer who will put stainless steel wire inside the ceramic."

"Or make the wire part separate from the cup? Like those plastic holders with the disposable cups inside of them? That idea led to problem three."

"It falls apart."

"Right." Samantha was thoroughly enjoying the problem-solving with Jack. She switched back to his original inquiry. "An inventor sees a need and attempts to provide a practical solution."

"Wait a minute," Jack protested, feeling as though he'd been reading a mystery that was missing the final pages. "What happened to the cup?"

"It's in one of the storage cabinets in the back. I got sidetracked by an airplane crash."

"Whoa! You were in a plane crash?"

She glanced over her shoulder in time to catch the flash of concern on his face. "Heaven's no! A customer mentioned the crash. Wouldn't it be wonderful if someone could invent a lightweight coating to spray on the underside of planes that would expand until it acted like a cushion for the plane when the landing gear didn't work?"

"That's what the model airplanes I saw littering the back room were for?"

"I pitched them last week. Too ambitious an undertaking. I know my limitations."

Watching the hem of her skirt rise as she stooped to dust the bottom shelves, level as she straightened, then rise again as she stretched to reach the top shelves, distracted him and he moved behind her. "Fascinating."

"My limitations?"

His arms closed around her waist. "Uh-uh. The way your skirt moves up and down while you work."

"Mr. Martin, shame on you." She snuggled back against him to take the sting out of the mild rebuke. "During business hours? Next think I know, you'll want me to flip the sign."

"You shouldn't rush into making radical changes in your business practices. Spoils the clientele." He lightly rotated his pelvis. "I'm interested in the inventor. You did tell me that the first thing an inventor does is assess a need, didn't you?"

"You catch on fast." She tilted her face upward and lightly kissed his jaw.

"Can't you think of a practical solution?"

From the corner of her eyes she saw Ralph peering in the window as he approached the door. She wiggled from Jack's light hold. "It's Ralph, the grocer. He's back to pick up the doll."

"Want me to hide in the back?" Jack teased, remembering the night they'd met. His presence and Ralph's untimely arrival had aggravated her.

"Pretend you're a customer. I may need your help."

"Uh-uh, lady," he said as he moved toward the back room. "This is your business. You run it."

Jack circled his thumb and forefinger into an "okay" signal and disappeared as the cowbell on the front door rang. *Have to be careful,* he thought, *to keep from treading on her sensitive toes.* It was one thing to make suggestions, but he wasn't going to shove them down her throat by watching her and giving her cues. He loved her sense of independence; he wasn't about to take it away from her.

Ralph entered the shop carrying a small sack. "My, oh, my," he gasped as his eyes roamed from one wall to the other. "How did you get the owners to renovate your shop?"

"You're looking at the renovator," Samantha replied, beaming Ralph a wide smile. "Look's great, doesn't it?"

"I'm astounded." Ralph scanned the orderly shelves until he spied his daughter's doll. "Did you get it fixed?'

"Certainly." Samantha shot a sly look toward the curtains dividing the shop from the back room. "How much did you pay for this nifty little doll?"

"Too much for an inefficient trash compactor." Ralph snorted a yuk-yuk laugh in her direction as she reached for the doll. "About forty dollars."

"Forty dollars?" Sam repeated, surprised Ralph would pay that much for a toy. "I'm in the wrong business. I should be inventing dolls that do what they're supposed to do."

Mentally she calculated a fair price for the repairs.

"That will be ten dollars," Samantha said in a brisk business voice.

Ralph's Adam's apple bobbed as he pushed the grocery sack toward her. "Ten dollars? In cash?"

Wondering if she was overcharging him, she was tempted to lower the price. Her eyes furtively slid toward the closed curtains. Darn it, she silently blasted toward the back room. This was Jack's idea. Why wasn't he there backing her up?

"Long green." She felt a tide of red threatened to creep from her neck to her forehead. Why did she feel so damned embarrassed? Ralph was a businessman. His customers paid cash.

"I brought you some fresh broccoli and cauliflower." Ralph poked the frames of his glasses with his forefinger, then pointed an accusing finger toward Samantha. He grabbed the doll by the head. "We've always traded food for repairs."

"Change of policy." She held the doll's feet firmly in her hands. The rubber doll's legs stretched. "Cash only."

Ralph's eyes narrowed. "No checks?"

"A check would be fine." Considering the time it had taken to locate the tube and to replace it, she shouldn't have felt guilty but she did. Much as she disliked cauliflower, she'd have eaten the whole thing raw rather than haggle with Ralph over money.

Why did she feel so rotten? Why didn't she let go of the doll's feet, grab the sack of groceries, and be thankful for the food? Because, she reminded herself, I earned the money. Ralph's wife would have thrown the doll away if it weren't for me.

With a snort, Ralph let go of the doll and reached in his slack's pocket for his checkbook. "Highway robbery. I didn't know robbers took checks."

Samantha grinned as she watched him fill out the check. In her usual friendly fashion, she teased, "Highwaymen like long green more than green vegetables, didn't you know?"

Ralph pursed his lips. "I don't know what prompted this change, but I don't like it," he huffed, tearing the check out of the book as though he wished he could do the same to Samantha. "Don't expect door-to-door delivery in the future."

Without another word, Ralph picked up the doll and the sack of groceries. Samantha cringed at the hostile look on his face. The door banged shut behind him.

"Thanks for the help," Samantha snapped toward the parting curtains.

Startled by her attack, Jack asked, "What did you want me to do?"

"You could have stayed out here and made a passing remark about what a good deal I gave him. Or you could have said something about sound business practices. What did you do? You hid!"

The look of dismay on her face brought Jack's protective instincts to the surface. Ralph wouldn't have any qualms about a foot-long cashier's tape. Why did the profit-motivated grocer object to Samantha making a profit?

"Ralph doesn't justify charging his customers." He leaned across the counter and lightly kissed her puckered forehead, wanting to erase the stress lines Ralph had caused. "You earned the money."

"Then why do I feel so rotten!" She clenched her fist and banged the countertop.

"Samantha, whatever you do is fine with me." Jack folded his hands over his fist. "Ralph is the one you should be angry with, not yourself. A head of cauliflower and a bunch of broccoli hardly qualifies as adequate compensation for the time you spent fixing the doll."

"But sometimes he brings groceries when I haven't fixed anything," she argued.

"He's taking advantage of your good nature. The only time you should feel guilty is when you get money for work you didn't do. He should have thanked you."

"He didn't," Samantha complained. "He hates me now."

"But he respects you. After he cools off, he'll admire the way you couldn't be intimidated."

"Do you really think so?" Her blue eyes misted at the thought of losing Ralph as a friend. She wasn't certain she wanted admiration more than she wanted friendship. Ten dollars was a meager price to put on friendship. "I know why people frame the first dollar they earn," Samantha grumbled, tempted to put Ralph's check in an envelope and mail it to him.

"Why?"

"Because it was the toughest dollar they ever earned."

She looked so wounded, so vulnerable that Jack wanted to fold her under his protective wing and shield her. But he knew if he cocooned her from a slight reproof, when he wasn't around, she'd regress to letting people like Ralph take advantage of her sweetness.

"It'll get easier. Changes in policy are always rough at first." He smiled his encouragement. "Look at the bright side. Money isn't just an obnoxious piece of paper issued by the government. It's capital to finance your next project."

Sam gave him a small smile.

"While you're becoming a financial wizard, I'll do what I can to market your inventions. You take care of the cash register, and I'll draft a letter to send to a couple of men who should be interested in your inventions." He gently stroked her hand until it relaxed. "Together we're an unbeatable combination."

"You'll keep them from pirating my ideas, won't you?"

Grateful that her quick mind had gravitated away from Ralph and toward protecting the patent rights on her inventions, he chuckled, "Oh, ye of little faith. Reputable companies don't invent around an idea. You refused to sign the standard release form that O'Toole's sent you, didn't you?"

Her chin raised a fraction of an inch. "I've heard some real horror stories."

"About inventors who had their ideas lifted by the big, bad corporate wolves? Honey, that's the reason you have to sign the waiver form. In nine out of ten cases, the courts rule in favor of the company simply because one of their research scientists has been working on the product."

"Coincidence?"

Jack gestured to her lithograph of Alexander Graham Bell that hung on a side wall. "He invented the telephone. Did you know another man presented an application to the patent office the same day Bell presented his? The courts decided in Bell's favor. That isn't an isolated coincidence. Why do you think Nobel prize winners in Russia have shared awards with Americans?''

"Because they both came up with the same idea," Samantha replied. Still a bit paranoid about someone stealing her inventions, she tapped her forehead. "What's up here can't be stolen."

"Or sold."

"Then I'll save up the money I earn from the Fixit Shop and manufacture the products myself. Then I'll get all the money."

"How much do you know about cost analysis? Net profit? Gross worth? Tooling machines? Labor practices? Invoices?''

Shaking her head, she held up her hands in submission.

"A shrewd businessman would love to see you struggle with such a company. If you did have a marketable product, the moment you started bankruptcy procedures, he'd come along and buy your company for a song. That, my dear, is where the real piracy occurs."

"Not with you helping me."

"Sorry. A doctor doesn't operate on members of his family and I don't manage a fledgling company for a woman I care about."

"But I trust you!"

"Now that's a prime example of an illogical, intuitive decision. Why do you trust me?"

Sam grinned. Anyone could look at Jack and see that he was straight as an arrow from his conservative haircut right down to his wing-tip shoes. "It's because I know you care about me."

"Some smooth-talking charlatan would love to get to know you."

"Tom the Thief," she muttered to herself.

Jack observed the flash of pain narrowing her eyes. "Who?"

"A man I once knew. He stole an idea. The dumb part is that I would have given it to him if he'd asked for it."

"Another reason you're shy about trusting men?"

"I guess," she admitted, ducking her head, recalling Tom's empty promises of undying love. "Some lessons hurt more than others."

"Do you trust me enough to let me go through those new filing cabinets of yours and write letters of inquiry for you?"

"I trust you."

"That's a beginning," Jack said, sealing the fragile bond with a loving kiss.

# Ten

———

You can't make chicken salad out of chicken scratchings," Samantha commented later that afternoon as she watched Jack decipher her illegible handwriting.

Intermittently throughout the day she'd peeked between the curtains to see what he was doing. He'd pored over her letters of inquiry and the corresponding letters of rejection. Until she interrupted him, he'd been thumbing through the pages of her daily journal.

A slow, heartwarming smile lit his face. He looped his arm around Samantha's waist and pulled her on his lap. "Speaking of chicken salad, I'm starved," he hinted.

"P.B. and J.?"

"Hamburgers!"

"Mom's dinner spoil your taste for peanut butter?" she jibed.

"No, but man cannot live by peanut butter alone. I need meat, potatoes, salad!" Jack sniffed. "What's that heavenly smell?"

"Hamburgers! French fries! Salad with French dressing."

"Nourishment. Lead the way."

Within minutes Jack had her work space cleared of papers, and Samantha emptied the white bags in front of him.

"From the sound of the cowbell on the door, I'd guess that you've been busy?"

"The cash register has more in it than we do. Help yourself. Can I get you a longneck?"

"Beer?"

"Dallas city-slickers," she chided. "Of course I meant a beer."

"I listened to your conversation with Melissa." Jack tilted the chair back on its rear legs and teased, "I figured if you could take care of her problem, you might be asking me if I want my neck stretched."

"Your neck is perfect," she complimented him, valiantly trying to switch the topic of conversation away from Melissa's boobs.

"Exactly what are you designing for Melissa?"

Samantha sat down and unwrapped her hamburger. She took a king-size bite and chewed it at great length. When Jack prodded her for an answer she pointed to her mouth.

"A bra," she finally answered, swallowing. "That's what those weird designs on the last pages of the logbook are."

"I thought you were designing suspension bridges."

Sam grinned. "It's sort of the same principle."

"Isn't one of those cross-your-heart contraptions adequate for Melissa?"

"You heard her leave. What do you think?"

"From the sounds I heard, the cowbell must have fallen to the floor from the impact of her slamming the door."

She dipped a french fry in the container of mustard and popped it into her mouth. "It did. She had this wild idea that the size and shape of her breasts influences her chances of becoming a star."

"That's ridiculous. The majority of starlets would envy Melissa's well-endowed figure."

"My sentiments exactly." Her eyes bounced from her front to the french fries Jack was smothering with ketchup, then back to her breasts.

"Yours are beautiful," Jack said, seeing the doubt clouding her face. He cupped his palm. "Perfect."

To cover her flustered state, she wiped her mouth with a paper napkin. "I told Melissa designing a special bra was a frivolous waste of my time. She insisted. I told her I'd charge her an hourly rate."

"Melissa hit the roof."

"The cowbell," Samantha corrected. "Intentionally. I think she'd like to have thrown it at me." Sam couldn't talk about the initial reaction of her friend. Melissa's face had dropped at the mention of money changing hands. Neither of them had a surplus of funds. That fact, coupled with Sam's faith in her friend's acting ability, made refusing to work on a special design doubly difficult.

The bell hitting the floor signaled more than Melissa's departure. Sam had physically felt something shrivel up inside her. Operating expenses and capital were important, but . . .

"What are you thinking? You're closing me out, Samantha."

"To be frank, I'm not certain I'm built to be a business tycoon," she solemnly admitted.

"You're perfect in every way. If you feel uncomfortable charging your close friends for your work, then don't."

"Easier said than done. How do I explain to the baker that he had to pay, but the grocer doesn't?" She sipped the beer. It tasted flat. "Sentimentality goes on the debit side of the ledger. I'll have to toughen up."

Jack put his half-eaten sandwich back in its wrapper. "Samantha, I don't want you to change, to get tough. Isn't there a happy middle ground? One where you can live in orderly financial comfort without feeling guilty?"

"I'm a person of extremes. Good or bad, I do everything whole hog."

He tugged the curl in the middle of her forehead, remembering a nursery rhyme from his early childhood. "Blame your new business practices on me. I'll be your official complaint department."

"That's sweet of you to offer, but..." she sighed heavily, "I'm determined to run this business as a profit-making organization. I bank the money, so I have to take responsibility for any disgruntled customers."

"Don't go overboard." He took her hand and brought it to his lips. Remembering she couldn't swim, he added, "You'll be in over your head before you know it."

"I've been wading knee-deep in a shallow pool for years." Wading? *Waiting,* she corrected silently. Waiting for a man like Jack. Waiting to sell an invention. Waiting to save up enough capital to finance projects.

She wouldn't wait any longer. "My baby-pool days are over. With your help, I'll make the Olympic swim team."

Jack heard the firm, resolved tone of her voice. What bothered him was the sad droop of her delectable mouth. She'd admitted to being a person of extremes. What he needed to do was help her attain some moderation. Balancing her life would take her on a direct path to the gold medals.

His thumb twisted the garnet ring on her fourth finger until only a thin, narrow gold band could be seen. Something wider, he thought, considering what type of wedding band would suit her. Samantha's long, tapered fingers wrapped around his thumb.

His dark eyes narrowed. Wedding ring? Marriage? He'd always thought changing his status from bachelor to husband the most radical of changes. Now he realized that Samantha wasn't the only one changing, adapting, reorganizing their way of thinking.

"Eat," he instructed, squeezing her fingers, then releasing them. "What time do you plan on closing the shop today?"

Wrapping the remains of her sandwich, Samantha shoved it back into the sack and tidied up. "It's closed. There isn't much action around here after two o'clock."

"We could go over your logbook together."

Sam started to brush the crumbs on the floor. Instead, she swished them to the edge of the table with the sack and brushed them into the waste basket. "The creative juices aren't flowing."

"There must be some productive way we can spend a long, lazy afternoon together."

She heard a wistful note in his voice, saw his eyes drift toward the sofabed. "You haven't cleaned up your mess,'' she said, watching him rise to his feet, stretch, then move to the bed.

''Everything in moderation, love. Come 'ere.''

''You're not helping me reform.''

''True.''

''You don't care about half-eaten food being left on the table?''

''Not in the least bit. Come here, Samantha. Let's see if I can get those creative juices flowing again.'' He stretched out on the bed, folding his hands behind his head, crossing his ankles. His eyes shut as he thought of inventive ways to make love with Samantha.

''It'll just take a minute.'' She hurriedly cleared the table. The smell of burgers and fries lingered in the air. She crossed to the cabinet below the sink to get the room freshener. Everything had to be perfect for Jack.

''You're going in the wrong direction,'' Jack said, wondering why she was rummaging around under the sink.

Samantha pulled the cap off the deodorizer and liberally spritzed it around the room. ''Isn't that better?''

''Terrific,'' he replied, holding his hand toward her.

She put the can back under the sink. ''I'll be there in just a second.''

''Samantha, what are you doing?''

''I put my toothbrush and toothpaste in here.''

''We both had the same kind of sandwich.''

''I know.'' She peeked over the cabinet door. ''I have an extra toothbrush if you'd like to use it. A razor, too.''

Jack rubbed his palm over his unshaven jaw. ''Are you hinting that I need to brush my teeth and shave?''

Afraid she'd offended him, she shook her head. ''I'm sorry. I thought . . .''

Leaping from the sofa bed, Jack crossed the room. He grabbed her shoulders and brought her to her feet. "I don't give a damn about deodorizers or peppermint breath."

His lips swooped down, crushing her surprised gasp to the back of her throat and changing it to a small gurgle of desire as his tongue darted back and forth across the roof of her mouth. She dropped the toothbrush in her hand, much preferring to hold him.

Jack waltzed her back to the bed. His fingers busily unbuttoned her shirt. He peeled it over her shoulders. "I've thought of a delightful way to make use of these whiskers."

"How?" Samantha shed her remaining clothing, as did Jack.

"Lay down on your tummy. I'll scratch your back."

"How did you know I love having my back scratched?" she asked as she did his bidding. The mattress shifted as he positioned his knees on either side of hers.

"Male intuition." He bent over her, brushing the short bristles on his jaw from one shoulder blade to the other. "Feel good?"

"Mmmm. Right across my bra line, please. Heavenly, absolutely heavenly. What every woman needs..."

He lifted her shoulders enough to allow his hands to massage her breasts as he followed her spine from her nape to the three intriguing dimples below her waist. She shivered in ecstasy as he lavishly kissed each indentation.

"You aren't thinking about sharing this discovery with other women are you?" he asked, when he heard her nails raking the pillowcase.

"I'm not thinking about anything." Which was the surprising truth. "I'm mindless putty in your hands."

Sam, the inventor, vanished.

Sam, the woman, squirmed until she rolled over, inviting him to rub her front as thoroughly as he'd rubbed her back.

His whiskered cheeks discovered the soft underside of her breasts. Her nipples pearled, coming alive, vibrating as his moist tongue circled them.

"Jack," she breathed, when his jaw rasped up her throat to her ear, her cheek. And finally, he fitted his lips over hers. He kissed her again and again, tenderly, harshly, until her face burned with heat. He persisted in tormenting her inch by inch. She felt as though he'd painted a trail of silken fire over her. She moaned, moving beneath him. His name became a litany of her love. He paused only long enough to protect her. "Jack, Jack..."

She pulled his hips to hers, grinding, arching, seeking the fulfillment he could give. His fingers dug into her sweet flesh. Unable to deny her or himself, he thrust inside her.

"I'm about to explode," she whispered huskily.

Their lips ground together, their tongues fueling the thrust of his hips, the arch of her back, until passion burst between them.

Jack collapsed by her side, gulping for air. She curled against him, burrowing her face in his shoulder. Neither of them could speak for long moments.

Finally, with a shaky chuckle, Samantha whispered, "I never knew a back rub could be so thrilling."

Feathering his fingers through her damp curls, his eyes closed in lazy contentment, he smiled. "Just a sample of my creative juices."

During the next several weeks, the hot Texas sun sizzling the paved street outside the shop compared poorly with the growing fever of Samantha's passion for Jack. The sweltering hot days she spent in her air-conditioned shop tending to business and daydreaming about him. The nights they spent together, sometimes at her place, other times at his. They reserved Sundays for her parents.

Samantha perched herself on the tall stool behind the counter and stared aimlessly out the front window. Last night, after dining at her parents' house, Jack had told her he was leaving Monday after work to go to O'Toole's general headquarters in Austin. He hadn't been gone twenty-four hours, but Samantha missed him sorely.

She glanced from the calendar on the wall to the ledger beside the cash register. Silently she chastised herself for sitting around doing nothing when she should have been busy tallying the month's receipts. She also had an inventory of items that had been left in the shop for over thirty days that she needed to return. And if thinking about those chores wasn't enough to get her off her rear end and get her busy, she had a stubborn computer printer in the workroom that refused to double space.

Yawning at the tedious list of chores, she strummed her fingers lazily on the countertop. They could wait. It had been weeks since she'd enjoyed the luxury of simply sitting and thinking. She told herself she wasn't bored, but a little irate devil inside her reminded her that she hadn't worked on any of her projects for weeks.

"Don't have time," she said to herself. The irony struck her. "You're sitting here doing nothing and you don't have time?"

Lack of inclination, she silently revised. Her mind constantly buzzed with numbers instead of with brilliant flashes of genius. She shrugged dismissively, but her stomach lurched. Now that she thought about it, she hadn't been on a creative binge in months.

Jacob, waving a magazine as he walked into the shop, distracted her from her introspection. Of all her so-called friends, he was the only one who hadn't complained about the change in policy regarding money.

"Hey lady! Congratulations!"

"On what? Being lazy?"

"What do you mean on what? Haven't you seen the advertisement in *Southern Fishermen*?" He opened the magazine to the place by his finger. He read aloud, "O'Toole Life Preservers, Inc., will proudly present a revolutionary new product this fall. Be prepared to fish in the comfort of a new streamlined life jacket and hip boots. Mae West save your life? O'Toole saves it without Mae's extra padding!"

"Let me see that." Sam scanned the ad, which showed a voluptuous caricature of Mae West. Only she wasn't wearing the standard life jacket. Her curves were fitted into skintight versions of a life jacket and hip boots. Sam ripped the centerfold from the magazine. "I don't believe it!"

"What?"

"They invented around SAM trunks! Those skunks must have figured they couldn't sell the public on the trunks, so they took the fabric and bastardized it into... *this*!" She wadded the offensive pages into a tight ball and pitched it against the far wall.

"You don't think Jack..."

The question Jacob was unable to complete hung between them in tense silence.

"Of course not," they chorused together.

"Jack wouldn't do that to me," Samantha added, but the suspicion lingered.

Her stricken eyes rose to the lithograph of Alexander Graham Bell. Was this going to be another coincidence? Did the research lab at O'Toole Life Preservers just happen to be working on a new fabric at the same time she'd designed the trunks? Or had Jack taken his autographed trunks to the lab and had the fabric analyzed?

"Of course he wouldn't," Jacob agreed. "Jack wouldn't betray you."

"I trusted him." Her voice dropped to a whisper. "I trusted Tom the Thief, too."

"Aw, come on Sam, Jack wouldn't do that."

Samantha felt physically ill. Her stomach clenched as tightly as her fist. Swallowing, she tasted salty tears. Her legs threatened to buckle as she moved to the display window. "Any one could have slipped a pair out of here."

Her voice cracked. The other pairs remained neatly arranged where she'd displayed them. Jack had the only missing pair.

"There has to be an explanation." Jacob slung his arm clumsily across her shoulder and pulled her against his chest.

"Money. Cold, hard cash." Sam gulped. Samantha had said the words, but she didn't believe them. Jack wasn't another Tom. She trusted Jack, loved him. His integrity, his honesty were two of the sterling qualities she admired in him. They couldn't be a sham. Oh, God, she silently prayed, don't let this happen. Please!

Jacob was as stunned as Sam. "I don't believe it. Where is he?"

"In Austin. General Offices." She leaned away from Jacob and stared into his troubled eyes. The circumstantial evidence, too damning to be ignored, made her drop her head as unchecked tears silently slid down her cheeks. "Tell me he didn't do it, Jacob."

The cowbell clanged. Jacob turned and made a shooing motion with his hand at Melissa.

Ignoring him, she marched into Sam's shop and brushed Jacob's hands away from Samantha's shoulders. "What's wrong?"

"Everything," Samantha sniffed. "I'm such a damned fool."

"What the hell is going on?" Melissa asked Jacob.

"I saw an O'Toole advertisement in *Southern Fisherman* for an innovative life preserver. I mistakenly jumped to the conclusion that Jack must have sold Sam's idea."

"Sam! How wonderful! I guess I must have been wrong about Jack after all," Melissa readily apologized. "You'll be rich!"

Jacob slapped his forehead at Melissa's obtuseness. "Sam didn't know a thing about it."

Her jaw dropping, Melissa froze. "Why that lousy heel. He's worse than those fake directors!"

"I can't believe he sold my invention," Samantha protested weakly.

"You can't? Well, sweetheart, love may be blind but the neighbors ain't!" Melissa glanced at Jacob. "Well, at least *some* of your neighbors aren't blind."

"Shut up, Melissa," Jacob ordered as he reached into his pocket for a handkerchief. "Here, Sam."

"I won't shut up. Jack Martin may be your ole school chum, but he isn't mine. Sam hasn't been the same since he showed up on the scene." Melissa consoled Sam by patting her on the back. With her other arm she gestured around the shop. "Just look at this place. Sterile as a hospital. Open from nine to five, six days a week. This isn't Sam's Fixit Shop!"

"No, it's a profitable business operation," Jacob replied, a snide edge to his voice. "Something Sam's so-called friends, who have taken advantage of her generosity, wouldn't understand."

"I ought to slap your face for that remark," Melissa threatened leaving Sam's side and advancing toward Jacob.

He raised his arm to protect himself. "This isn't the time for theatrics, Melissa."

Playing the role of defender of the innocent to the hilt, Melissa retorted, "I'm going to theatrics your pretty nose all over your ugly face!"

"Please, don't fight," Sam said, stepping between them. "I need all of my friends to get me through this. Right now, I'm going to call Austin and talk to Jack. I'd appreciate it if you'd both sit down and be quiet."

"I wouldn't talk to the rat," Melissa blustered.

Jacob handed Sam the phone. "*She's* being sensible!"

"Men!" Melissa grumbled, determined to have the last word.

"Actresses!" Jacob said.

"Florist!"

"That's enough!" Sam turned her back on both of them and punched the number to get long distance assistance. "Yes. I'd like the number of O'Toole Life Preservers's general office in Austin. Melissa, would you write this number down?"

"Hand me the pencil," Jacob ordered. "She'll get the number wrong."

"Go ahead, Sam," Melissa said, glaring at Jacob malevolently and whispering, "Go send yourself a dozen black roses."

Sam repeated the number aloud, then hung the phone back in its cradle. "What's wrong with you two?"

"She's in love with me and refuses to admit it," Jacob said, rolling his tongue in his cheek.

"I wouldn't love you if you were the last man on earth!"

Jacob snorted his disbelief. "Sam, you should have seen the steamy Valentine card she sent me. Wilted the vase of flowers I set it under."

"You ruined my hand-painted card?" For a second, Melissa's composure slipped. Drawing on her acting ability, she flicked an imaginary dust speck from the ruffle of her low-necked blouse. "You should have seen what I did to those heart-shaped balloons you sent. Like you, they popped because they were full of hot air."

"Hot air? You're the expert on being light-headed. I told you my going to Sam's house for dinner didn't mean a damned thing. But, oh, no, you were practicing for the role of some half-crazy, jealous loony, and wouldn't believe me. Dammit, I told you I loved you."

Samantha's eyes ping-ponged between her friends. Her ears must be playing tricks on her. Jacob loved Melissa? She'd never suspected anything had gone on between the two of them other than hostility.

"You and Melissa?" she gasped, forgetting her major crisis. "In love?"

"Not any more," Melissa replied. Her chin wobbled ever so slightly but enough for Jacob to notice.

"Not any less," he corrected. "Sam, tell her the truth about the Sunday dinner."

"I coerced Jacob into eating Sunday dinner at my parents' house to make my parents happy. Honest Melissa, I didn't know!"

Jacob ploughed his hand through his hair. "And I accepted because Melissa kept baiting me with those producers."

"*Fake* producers, in more ways than one," Melissa confessed. "They never existed."

Samantha watched relief flood Jacob's face. At the last moment his mouth twisted sardonically.

"What about the night I saw you flirting with Jack Martin?" he asked, demanding an explanation. "You practically—"

"I saw you watching from your store. I thought I'd give you a whiff of how it feels to be jealous."

Jacob grinned. His homeliness became obscured by the love beaming in his amber eyes. "Homely men are experts on jealousy. Think I could convince you to be my leading lady?"

Samantha watched Melissa leap into Jacob's arms. Samantha moved toward the back room. "Speaking of Jack Martin, would you two excuse me? I have a phone call to make."

Her friends' unexpected happiness magnified her difficulties. Always a bridesmaid, never a bride, she predicted.

What had gone wrong?

She'd changed.

The shop was squeaky clean. Her bookkeeping was something a C.P.A. would envy. Her thoughts centered solely around Jack. She'd given him everything—her heart, her love and unlimited access to her logbook. What had she gotten in return?

She wiped a single tear from her cheek and held it on her fingertip, examining it. By Jack's standards, she hadn't been a success when he first met her. But she remembered being genuinely happy. She hadn't shed a tear in years. And now, with all the changes she'd made, all her success business wise, she was crying.

"Serendipity Samantha where are you?" she whispered, glancing down at the clothes Jack had helped her choose to wear in the shop.

She stripped off the floral print jacket and flung it toward the sofa. The skirt and matching blouse quickly followed. She dug in the bottom of her dresser drawer and retrieved a pair of faded jeans and an ancient tie-dyed top. She held the clothes in front of her.

This was Serendipity Sam's uniform.

She'd tried to conform, to be what Jack wanted. She'd contorted her free spirit into his rigid, unyielding mold. Free-flowing lines can't be fitted into a neat, square hole. She'd only been fooling herself by trying to be something *Jack* had invented.

She slipped on her clothes. They fit like a familiar glove.

There was one major flaw in Jack's invention, she realized all too late. Her years of discarding useless pieces and parts that didn't work came into focus. Jack had squeezed and shaped her into an astute business woman, but the woman he'd initially wanted had been discarded piece by piece.

She was an inventor who hadn't had a single idea since being revamped.

Jack had been smarter than she had. He'd seen her lack of productivity, and like a worthless part, he'd pitched it.

She'd changed for the worse.

"I am what I am," she said.

She glanced at the phone hanging on the wall. She couldn't call him. Whether innocent or guilty of stealing her idea, it didn't matter. He hadn't deceived her; she had deceived herself.

Sam walked to the drawing board and flipped her daily log open. No entries had been made since the night she'd spent at Jack's condo. Whatever mental block she'd barricaded her creativity behind disintegrated as she traced the electrical diagram of her Turn Out the Light contraption with her finger.

Dusk turned to darkness, darkness to dawn. The Closed sign remained on her door. The small prototype of her invention flicked the light on and off. Sam hadn't perfected Samantha, but she had perfected her invention.

# Eleven

---

Feeling higher than the clouds the airplane flew above, Jack silently congratulated himself on his good fortune—Samantha's good fortune. Donald O'Toole, President of O'Toole Life Preservers, Jack mused, was reputed to be older than God and meaner than the devil. For a second, Jack almost pitied the marketing team that had promised to deliver an exciting new product but failed.

During the past weeks, he'd heard rumbles about the plans to update O'Toole life jackets with a revolutionary new fabric. He'd sent a letter of inquiry to headquarters regarding *Save-A-Man* trunks. Rather than raise Samantha's hopes, he'd kept quiet. Like Samantha, he'd received a rejection slip.

He grinned. Dear Samantha, laboring in her cluttered, unscientific, penny-pinching shop, had proven herself a veritable genius. Or so Mr. O'Toole had said as he pounded Jack heavily on the back at the end of their private conference.

"A woman of foresight, me lad," O'Toole had complimented her in his thick Irish brogue. "Combined with independence, guts and fortitude."

Jack could have added beautiful and sexy as hell.

O'Toole had offered a considerable sum for an outright purchase of the pending patent. Taking a page out of Samantha's book, Jack had refused. This was Samantha Ann Mason's invention. She'd want the credit. By damned, he'd see that she got it. He'd taken a deep breath and stubbornly refused to negotiate anything other than a seven-year limited license on the bonding technique.

O'Toole had eyed him, threatened him, then laughed as he tentatively agreed and pounded Jack on his back.

Over dinner, O'Toole's piercing blue eyes had twinkled with amusement as Jack told him how he'd met Samantha. Both O'Toole and his wife were fascinated when they learned that Samantha couldn't swim a stroke.

Jack watched O'Toole pat his wife's hand when he told them about Samantha's creative binges. Later, Mrs. O'Toole shyly confessed to holing up at their lake house for days on end when she was painting. Just as Samantha visualized practical improvements to make life easier, Mrs. O'Toole dreamed of paintings that would give their owners a slice of life's beauty. O'Toole's pride in his wife's accomplishments matched Jack's pride in Samantha.

Jack glanced at the overhead Fasten Seat Belt sign and waited for it to light up. He was anxious to get back to Samantha and break the good news.

For a second, his brow puckered. He'd been gone a week. He'd phoned each evening but no one had answered. Sharing the excitement with her would have been the icing on the cake. Worried, he'd called Jacob and Melissa to have them check on Samantha. He hadn't been able to reach them either.

He rubbed his stomach. Airplane food mixed with high altitude invariably caused indigestion problems, he thought, excusing the knotting sensation.

The feeling didn't abate. If anything, by the time he reached the shopping center, it had increased in intensity.

Jack parked the car in front of the Fixit Shop. "What's the Closed sign doing on the door?" he muttered, confused by the change in routine.

Something was wrong. Dreadfully wrong. What could have happened?

He sprinted to the door. The sun's glare kept him from seeing inside until he cupped his hands around his eyes. Once, then twice, he blinked, unable to believe his eyes. The place was a disaster area. Worse than when he'd first seen it.

He raised his hand to pound on the plate glass, but stopped himself. Undoubtedly Samantha had hooked up the growling lion. He let out a roar of his own, "Samantha! Unlock the door!"

Dammit, she was in there. He could see a sliver of light coming from under the curtain covering the doorway to the back room.

"Open up, Samantha! I'm home."

Silence. The curtain remained closed. He'd have to go through Jacob's flower shop to get to the back entrance.

The combination of jogging the short distance to the flower shop and the gut-level fear coursing through him had him panting as he entered Jacob's shop.

Melissa and Jacob were in a clinch that would have made the air roots on a philodendron envious.

Any other time, Jack would have whistled and teased them. But now only one thing was on his mind: Getting to Samantha. "Why's the Fixit Shop closed?" he demanded, heading for the aisle leading to the back door.

Jacob reached to his side and slammed the countertop down, barring Jack from the storage area. "Do I look like an information service?"

"Yeah, Jack," Melissa said, her eyes shooting daggers. "You want information? *Hire* a detective."

Exasperated, Jack stopped dead in his tracks. He raised his arms in a futile gesture. "I've been trying to contact Samantha or the two of you all week. What the hell is going on 'round here? In five short days have you all gone crazy?"

"I'd say we're all pretty normal. I think you're the one with the problem." Melissa propped her elbows on the counter, further blocking the path to the back door.

"Look, Melissa, I've had a hard week. Would you please step aside so I can go to the back entrance of Samantha's shop?"

"Sam doesn't want to see you," Jacob interjected. "What did you expect? We saw the O'Toole advertisement in the magazine. Are the new vests made of the same fabric as SAM trunks?"

"Maybe." His dark eyes narrowed as he speculated on what the three of them had thought when they saw the ad. "I didn't sell out on Samantha."

Melissa snorted her disbelief, rolling her eyes. "Roll up your trousers, Jacob. The bull he's putting out will be knee-deep soon."

"I'm not going to stand here and argue with you." He impaled Jacob with a chilly stare. "This is between me and Samantha. I'd appreciate it if you'd let me pass through your shop."

"Forget it, " Melissa answered for Jacob. "Sam's busy working on a wedding gift."

Glancing around the shop, Jack noticed the huge tropical plants had been replaced with orange blossom and honeysuckle arrangements. Elaborate bridesmaid bouquets hung on the walls. "Someone important getting married?"

Jacob grinned at Melissa. "We are."

"Unlike some people I know," Melissa added, "Jacob doesn't feel as though a woman has to *change* to be lovable."

"Any changes Samantha made were of her own choosing," Jack replied in his own defense. Then he asked, "When is your wedding?"

"Tomorrow. Samantha is the maid of honor," Jacob answered.

Locking her arm through the crook of Jacob's, Melissa cooed, "We'd invite you, but you might catch the bride's garter. I wouldn't wish you on any unsuspecting woman."

Jacob silenced Melissa by patting her hand. "You get things cleared up with Sam, which isn't likely, and you're welcome to attend."

"Thanks, Jacob. Can I cut through your shop?"

Nodding, the florist moved aside, taking Melissa with him. Jack quickly lifted the counter and skirted between the buckets of carnations, gladiolas and roses.

At least he wouldn't be totally off guard when he talked to Samantha. Here he'd thought she'd be delighted to hear his good news, but instead Sam and her friends believed he'd callously plotted to seduce Sam as a means to get his greedy hands on SAM trunks.

The truths they'd based their theory on were damning. From the moment he'd seen her, he'd itched to get his hands on Samantha. Every male hormone in his body had screamed her name. And he'd wanted O'Toole to license her invention. He couldn't deny any of that. The major flaw that marred their theory was that he hadn't wooed Samantha for mercenary reasons.

He loved Samantha.

Melissa had accused him of forcing Samantha to change. How many times had he told Samantha she didn't have to change to please him? She'd asked for his help. He'd given it. What should he have done? Say, "Sorry, sweetheart. I think a successful businesswoman is unfeminine. Stick to a diet of peanut butter and jelly until I ride in on a white horse and rescue you." For two cents, he would have told Melissa that changing Samantha's quirky habits was as unimportant to him as the shape of Melissa's bust was to Jacob.

He kicked an empty soda can down the alley. How could Samantha believe he'd steal from her? His fists rammed into his trouser pockets. His lungs heaved air like a bellows.

Believing what she believed, Jack knew she'd be steaming mad. No doubt the shop had taken the brunt of her wrath. So much for the wonderful surprise he'd expected to give her. A hurricane would be more welcome than his telling her he had sold the trunks.

"Control," he muttered, staring balefully at the metal door. Both of them couldn't ignite or there would be hell to pay. He'd lose Sam. She'd completely lose faith in herself as a woman. One of them had to be levelheaded.

Women weren't the only ones who could feel emotionally battered and bruised, he realized. Her lack of faith in him, regardless of the incriminating evidence, stung horribly.

Her back door opened before Jack worked up his courage enough to knock.

"Come in, Jack," Samantha invited him stiffly. He never could have known from the thrust of her chin, her voice, her rigid stance how much the mere sight of him affected her. If he hadn't betrayed her, she would have thrown her arms around his neck and hung on for dear life.

She'd spent all week meticulously planning everything. What she'd say. How he'd reply. The sale of SAM trunks wouldn't add to her coffers, but by damned she planned on having a fistful of revenge to fill the void.

She picked up the O'Toole advertisement from the table and waved it in his face. "I considered shredding this into confetti, but I didn't want to destroy the evidence."

Jack winced at her deliberate barb. Determined to cut through their complicated problems with swift precision, he bit back the angry retort on the tip of his tongue.

"I love you, Samantha," he said sincerely. "I've missed you."

Sam gasped at his audacity and flung the ad on the floor between them. The angry accusations she'd planned on whipping him with stuck in her throat. Dammit, it wasn't fair to disarm her attack with vows of love.

"That's a bit below the belt—even for a man who pilfers ideas from unsuspecting inventors."

Jack held his temper in check as her accusation flicked across his raw nerves. Her tones held the iciness of a blue norther, but he knew how vulnerable Tom the Thief had made her. Still, it galled him that she believed him capable of such an underhanded trick.

Hurting himself, he needled, "So is not trusting the man who is sharing your bed."

*Trust?* Samantha silently shrieked. Trusting Jack Martin was her first mistake. She'd trusted him with something far more valuable to her than SAM trunks. He'd taken advantage of that trust. All the time he'd been warning her about customers taking monetary advantage of her, he'd been busy stealing her heart.

Her bitter blue eyes clashed with his chocolate brown eyes. His didn't waver an inch. So much for liars not being able to look their victims in the eyes, she inwardly raged. Samantha tossed her head toward the sofa bed.

"Past tense. I'm trading in my double sofa bed for a twin-size bed." She gestured toward the brown paper sack by the door. "Your shaving kit is in there. Along with the remains of a box of Spic and Span. I won't be needing it once you're gone."

"Let me make certain I understand you. Are you suggesting that I'm the reason behind your cleaning binge?"

"Of course. I saw the way you looked down your nose at the clutter in here. My head may be up in the clouds most of the time, but—"

"I didn't ask you to scrub the shop. You did that on your own."

"But that's how you wanted everything, wasn't it? Spick-and-span? Ready for a white-glove test?"

His lips compressed, Jack shook his head. "I seem to recall telling you that I didn't want you to change. You're the one who flew off in a thousand and one directions."

"To please you." Samantha pointed her finger at him. "Why do you think I changed my whole way of life? Clutter never bothered me. I was content bartering services. But, oh, no! That wasn't right. Customers were taking advantage of me! I had to charge for fixing my friends' stuff."

Jack's lips flattened against his clenched teeth. "You asked for advice on business management. Charging your friends was your idea, not mine!"

"Uh-huh, sure it was," she replied sarcastically. "I guess it was my brainy idea to schedule my time so I'd be so busy I couldn't work on my projects, right?"

Samantha realized her accusation was unfair, but once she'd started babbling about how she'd changed her life to fit her concept of what he wanted in a woman, she couldn't stop. Like a windup toy, she continued along her destructive course. "You're the reason I haven't produced a single invention. I was busy. Busy making little signs. Busy setting up ledgers. Busy fixing, busy collecting, busy tallying profits."

Her chest heaved as she panted for air. Her heart pounded. Jack stood immobile. Her accusations and insults seemed to bounce off him without injury.

Jack's stomach turned inside out. If he'd been a less moderate man, he'd have grabbed her and shaken some

ense into her hard head. Only a small muscle along his
awline revealed his inner turmoil.

"That's what *you* wanted," he rebuked her softly.
"I'm in love with both of the women who live here.
Serendipity Samantha and Sam the inventress."

Covering her ears, blocking his lies, Samantha spun
oward the wall. Her words came in spurts between the
wisting pain centered around her heart. "Don't lie. You
lon't have to. I put a release form for the pending pat-
nt on the bonding process in the sack. It's a goodbye
ift. Dammit, take it and get the hell out of here."

"I didn't ask you to change," he reiterated. Stead-
astly he held on to the last shreds of his temper. "You
nade changes without consulting me. And I didn't steal
he trunks. You gave them to me."

Her blunt fingernails bit into the flesh of her palm.
The conversation wasn't going the way she'd planned.
When he realized he'd been caught with sticky fingers,
ne should have denied stealing her invention. Why
lidn't he tell her some cock-and-bull story? Why didn't
ne beg her forgiveness? Why was he standing behind
ner, acting as though he was the injured party, the per-
on suffering.

Jack reached into his suit pocket. "I have something
or you."

"I don't want anything from you, Jack Martin."
From the corner of her eye she saw an envelope land in
he middle of the bed.

"Don't you? Well, Samantha 'Sam' Mason, I want
omething from you."

"Just go to the display window and make your selec-
ion!" The voice she'd schooled to be haughty cracked.
'Why bother asking for anything you want?"

"Brilliant idea. A bonafide flash of genius." With th
width of the room like an icy crevasse between them, h
knew he wasn't going to get through to her. He move
close enough to place his hands lightly on her shoul
ders. "You're what I want."

Samantha inwardly jerked away from his touch. Bolt
of electricity kept her outwardly immobile, paralyzed
Only her bottom lip trembled uncontrollably. "I tol
you from the beginning it wouldn't work between us.'

"And then you set out to prove your theory. Yo
tested my persistence, my fortitude and now, my tem
per."

"They tested out solid as a rock," she admitted, fol
lowing his chain of thought.

"But when you boil it all down, you let an advertise
ment that I had nothing to do with tip the balance of th
scale against me." Jack rubbed his knuckles against th
thrust of her jaw. He sighed heavily. "It's a good thin
you are a woman. Otherwise I'd be tempted to knoc
your block off."

She saw the hard look in his eyes. Her chin droppe
fractionally. "You can't deny O'Toole wants the fab
ric."

"No. But I deny trying to sell it out from under you.'
His fingers threaded through the short curls of he
temple. "I'd heard rumbles being made in the market
ing department. Hell, Sam, I'll admit to sending a let
ter of inquiry to headquarters when I knew somethin
was up. Imagine how I felt when I got a standard rejec
tion slip. Anyway, when I went to Austin, I figured I'
be told the details. When I arrived, everyone was run
ning around like chickens with their heads cut off
Donnell O'Toole being the hatchet man."

Curiosity, coupled with a strong subconscious desire to vindicate Jack, made her ask, "Why?"

"Because, my dear inventress, someone had promised O'Toole something better than foam rubber to make life jackets with. Something thinner, more flexible."

"Something like the fabric in SAM trunks?"

"Exactly. I immediately suspected that someone at Astro Hall saw your live demonstration." His thumb languidly smoothed the wrinkles in her brow. "I tracked the idea back to Houston, but not to Astro Hall. Seems the space center had been making noises about a space-age fabric that had the strength of a bulletproof vest and the buoyancy of a cork. Anyway, *unofficial* wild promises were made. Meanwhile, O'Toole was certain the reports would change the industry. He started the ball rolling in the advertising department."

"The ad in *Southern Fisherman*?"

"Along with ads in several other national magazines. From what he said, I gather the text of the ad was vague, announcing a revolutionary new product, but nothing specific, right?"

Samantha nodded.

"All hell broke loose when the research reports arrived."

"And that's when you decided to show O'Toole the SAM trunks?'

"No. That's when I showed O'Toole the letter of inquiry I'd written and the formal letter of rejection I'd received. Then I showed him the trunks."

"Jack!" she wailed, reaching up and tugging his lapels. "What did he say?"

"First he muttered something about wasting a million-dollar advertising campaign." He put his hands on her shoulders as she began bounding up and down on her tiptoes.

"And then?"

"Then he asked me if they worked."

Sam landed on her heels. "They didn't work. I nearly drowned, remember?"

"You panicked. They worked fine on me. That's what I told O'Toole. All week they've been testing the fabric."

"Without my signing a release form? Jack! What if they invent around me? What if..."

He turned her face toward the sofa bed. "Read what's in the envelope."

She bounded to the center of the bed. Sitting Indian-fashion, she ripped open the envelope and pulled out the agreement. Her eyes scanned the pages. "Jack! They've agreed to... everything I wanted!"

"All the document needs is *your* signature." He grinned, his eyes dancing merrily as he watched her toss the sheets into the air.

"We did it! We're millionaires!" she crowed, standing in the middle of the bed. She lunged toward Jack. Her feet tangled in the blankets. She felt herself falling. "Jack!"

He was there, catching her, laughing, stringing kisses across her cheeks.

"Trust me?" he murmured, holding her tightly, loving the way she squirmed to get closer.

"I do...I did." Her nose burrowed into the crook of his neck. Her fingers dug into the suppleness of his broad shoulders. She wanted to cling and cling and cling and forget their other problems.

Her tenseness communicated to Jack. "Talk to me Samantha. Don't go spinning off into another world without me."

"I'm scared, Jack. I've tried to change to be what you want, but I can't."

"You are what I want." His fingers pushed through her thick, curly locks until they touched her scalp. "You don't need to change. You never have."

Sam sighed, loosening her hold. "I want to please you. But I can't win for losing. What makes you happy, makes me hate myself."

Although he still held her, Jack feared she would permanently slip away from him unless he finally discovered what made her tick. "Oh Lord, Samantha, the last thing I want to do is make you unhappy."

"It's not your fault. It's mine. In my mind, I know I should be businesslike, but in my heart, I don't give a damn about collecting money for fixing something." She raised her head to look him straight in the eye. "I'm back to the barter system with my friends. I just can't charge them."

"Then don't. I made *suggestions*, not *rules*."

"For anyone else, they make sense. But not for me." Disgruntled by her inability to adjust, she confessed, "I found myself charging for my services, then spending the rest of my time keeping track of how much time I spent repairing something, how much the parts cost, how much the item cost, how much interest I'd earn if I deposited the money in a savings account..." Her voice trailed off in the financial maze. "I can't be an astute businesswoman. The paperwork is like a paper towel blotting up my creative juices."

"That's what's really bothering you, isn't it? You narrowed your choices down to pleasing me or being an inventor?"

Samantha closed her eyes as she sadly nodded her head. Much as she loved Jack, she couldn't destroy herself to have him.

"That isn't a choice you have to make. Open those beautiful blue eyes of yours and look at me." Her lids fluttered open warily. "Sam, I love *you*. Hire a book-keeper...close the shop...convert my condo into a workshop. I don't care what you do as long as you love me."

"Jack, I can't live a spotless life," she whispered, her defenses crumbling under the lovelight shining in his dark eyes. "I care more about letting my thoughts flow than watching mop water flood the floor."

"Hire a cleaning woman. That's what I do."

She grabbed him by the ears. "You mean you don't keep your condo scrubby-dub all by yourself?"

"I never said I did. You never asked."

"But I thought..." Her voice trailed away into nothingness as his smiling lips curved over hers. His kiss was brief, close-mouthed, unsatisfying. "I thought—"

"You do a lot of thinking, Sam. I don't want that to change, either. The only replicas of myself will be created two or three years down the road after we're an old married couple."

Samantha heard the lilt in his voice. "Virgos. Conceived in love, delivered in September," she promised.

"Twins, maybe? Sam and Samantha?"

Grinning from ear to ear, she hugged him. "I'm not certain I'd wish that on anybody," she said with a mock groan. "Although their grandparents would say I deserved everything I got."

Her mind took flight. She imagined having Jack's sons and daughters. Dark hair, dark eyes, charming, industrious, fastidious . . .

"I love you, Samantha." he searched her far-away expression, looking for signs of mechanical inspiration. He looked for one thing but found another. Her bright eyes held only love.

"And I love you, Jack. From the bottom of my heart to my serendipity brain."

# Silhouette Desire

## COMING NEXT MONTH

**IN EVERY STRANGER'S FACE—Ann Major**
Jordan Jacks had made his way into Gini's heart years before, but their
different life-styles forced her away from him. Whether she wanted it or not, he
was back in her life, and this time their desire couldn't be denied.

**STAR LIGHT, STAR BRIGHT—Naomi Horton**
The only heavenly bodies astronomer Rowan Claiburn was interested in were of
the celestial variety. But Dallas McQuaid made an impressive display, and she
found this man who radiated sex appeal impossible to ignore.

**DAWN'S GIFT—Robin Elliott**
Creed Parker fled from his dangerous, fast-paced world for the country life, but
his peace of mind was shattered when he saw beautiful Dawn Gilbert emerging
from her morning swim. Could Creed's past allow him to accept Dawn's gift of
a future?

**MISTY SPLENDOR—Laurie Paige**
Neither a broken engagement nor time could quell the passion between Misty
and Cam. She had left because they hadn't been ready for marriage—but now
as man and woman they were ready for love.

**NO PLAN FOR LOVE—Ariel Berk**
Brian Hollander's "Casanova" style was cramped when he had to play
surrogate daddy to his newborn nephew. Valerie knew even less about babies
than Uncle Brian, but her labor of necessity turned into a labor of love.

**RAWHIDE AND LACE—Diana Palmer**
After Erin left Ty her life fell to pieces; then an automobile accident ruined her
career. Now Ty wanted her back, for Erin held the key to his happiness. Could
she give her heart again to the man who had once turned her away?

## AVAILABLE THIS MONTH:

**TREASURE HUNT**
Maura Seger

**THE MYTH AND THE MAGIC**
Christine Flynn

**LOVE UNDERCOVER**
Sandra Kleinschmit

**DESTINY'S DAUGHTER**
Elaine Camp

**MOMENT OF TRUTH**
Suzanne Simms

**SERENDIPITY SAMANTHA**
Jo Ann Algermissen

## Silhouette Desire

**Available
October 1986**

# California Copper

The second in an exciting new
Desire Trilogy by Joan Hohl.

If you fell in love with Thackery—the
laconic charmer of *Texas Gold*—you're
sure to feel the same about his twin
brother, Zackery.

In *California Copper*, Zackery meets the
beautiful Aubrey Mason on the windswept
Pacific coast. Tormented by memories,
Aubrey has only to trust... to embrace
Zack's flame... and he can ignite the fire in
her heart.

The trilogy continues when you
meet Kit Aimsley, the twins' half
sister, in *Nevada Silver*. Look for
*Nevada Silver*—coming soon from
Silhouette Books.